monica ©

Adventures

Mauricio

#2
WE FOUGHT EACH
OTHER AS KIDS...
NOW WE'RE
IN LOVE?!

charmZ
NEW YORK

Monica

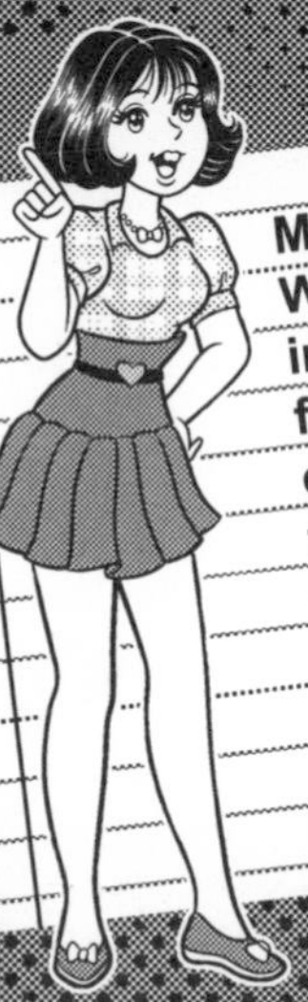

Monica is a sweet, happy, buck-toothed, teenage girl. When she was younger, she was known for being intolerant of disrespect and always stood up for her friends. That is, unless Jimmy-Five and Smudge would cause her trouble, then Monica would bash them with her favorite plush blue bunny, Samson! Still, occasionally, she does her classic bunny bashings as a teen, but has chilled out when it comes to Jimmy-Five, who has been catching her attention a lot more lately. Monica is the leader of the gang because of her honest and charismatic—and powerful—personality.

J-Five

Jimmy-Five, or J-Five, has always been picked on for his speech impediment. He used to lisp, which caused him to switch letters around, such as r's for w's, when he would speak. He has grown out of that as a teen, unless he's nervous, which typically happens around a certain girl. He also was picked on because of the five strands of hair he had on his head, which have all sort of filled out as a teen. Still, J-Five is sometimes made fun of for his hair, but he doesn't let it get to him as much anymore! When J-Five was young, he would often try to steal Monica's blue bunny from her and attempt to take over as leader of the gang with his questionable schemes. J-Five is no longer focused on being head of the gang as much as he's focused on being close with his friends, and closer to one friend in particular…

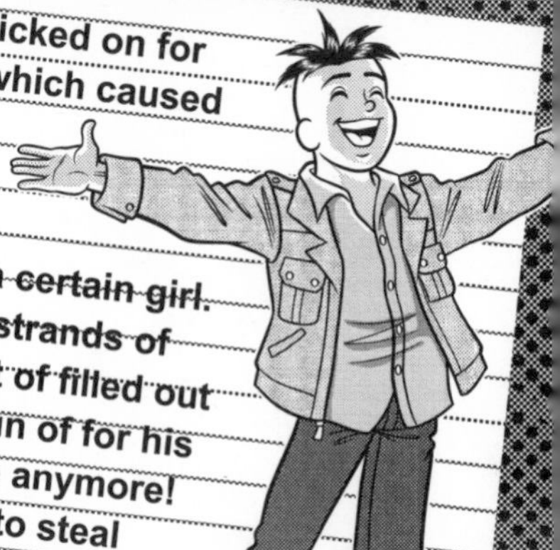

Smudge

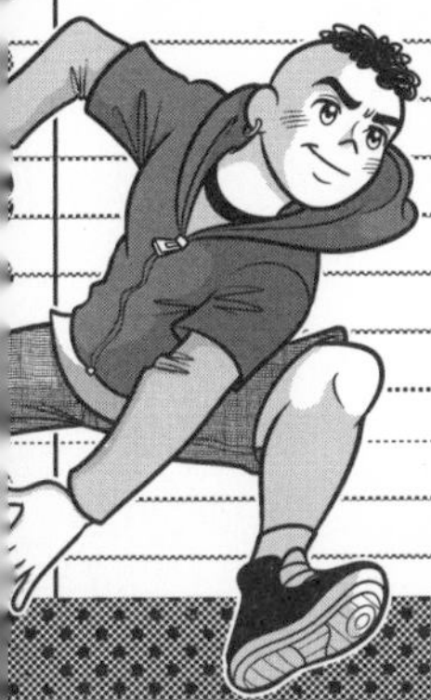

Smudge has never liked water and prefers his messy and dirty lifestyle over showers, rain, swimming, or even drinking water any day, but he's warmed up to taking showers as a teen… sort of. He cleans up sometimes mainly because the opinion of girls has started to matter to him, unlike when he was a kid. Smudge loves sports, especially skateboarding and soccer because of how radical they are. He also loves comics, and shares this love with his best friend, J-Five! Smudge is kind of the "handyman" of the gang, always helping his friends in times of need but typically also messing everything up.

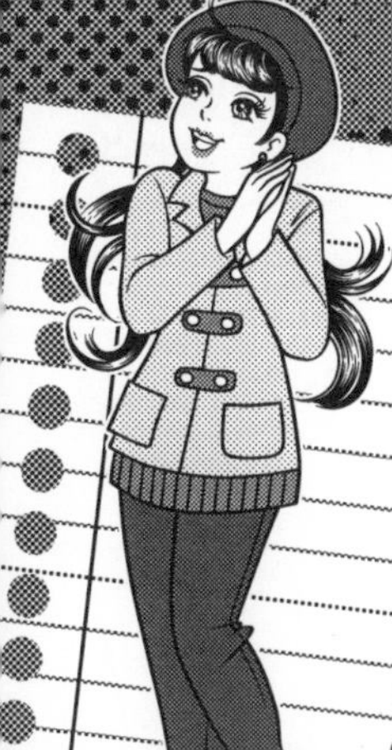

Maggy

Maggy is Monica's best friend, always having her back and being there for her in good times and bad. Maggy is also a huge lover of cats. Maggy has always had a voracious appetite, mostly eating watermelons but never discriminating against any other food put in front of her. Maggy is more conscious of what she eats now… perhaps a little too much. She is virtually obsessed with proper nutrition, sports, and exercise instead of eating anything she sees.

#2 "We Fought Each Other as Kids...Now We're in Love?!"

Characters, Story, and Illustration created by MAURICIO DE SOUSA
ZAZO AGUIAR, MARCELA CURAC RUSSI, and FELIPPE BARBIERI—Cover Artists
MAURICIO DE SOUSA, MARINA TAKEDA E SOUSA, PETRA LEÃO—Script
DENIS Y. OYAFUSO, JOSÉ APARECIDO CAVALCANTE, LINO PAES, ROBERTO M. PEREIRA—Pencils
MAURO SOUZA, ZAZO AGUILAR—Illustrations
CRISTINA H. ANDO, JAIME PODAVIN, ROSANA G. VALIM, TATIANA M. SANTOS, VIVIANE YAMABUCHI, and WELLINGTON DIAS—Inks
MARCELO CASSARO—Lettering
A. MAURICIO SOUSA NETO—Finishes
JAE HYUNG WOO, FÁBIO ASADA, MARCELO KINA, MARIA JÚLIA S. BELLUCCI—Colorists
MARIA DE FÁTIMA A. CLARO—Art Coordination
SANDRO ANTONIO DA SILVA—Script Supervisor
ALICE K. TAKEDA—Executive Director
SIDNEY GUSMAN—Editorial Planner
ÍVANA MELLO, SOLANGE M. LEMES—Original editors
PECCAVI TRANSLATIONS—Original Translations

Special thanks to LOURDES GALIANO, RODRIGO PAIVA, MÔNICA SOUSA, and MAURICO DE SOUSA

JEFF WHITMAN—Editor, Production
KARR ANTUNES—Editorial Intern
JIM SALICRUP
Editor-in-Chief

Charmz is an imprint of Papercutz.
PB ISBN: 978-1-5458-0216-8
HC ISBN: 978-1-5458-0217-5
Printed in China
January 2019

Charmz books may be purchased for business or promotional use.
For information on bulk purchases please contact Macmillan
Corporate and Premium Sales Department at
(800) 221-7945 x5442

Distributed by Macmillan
First Charmz Printing

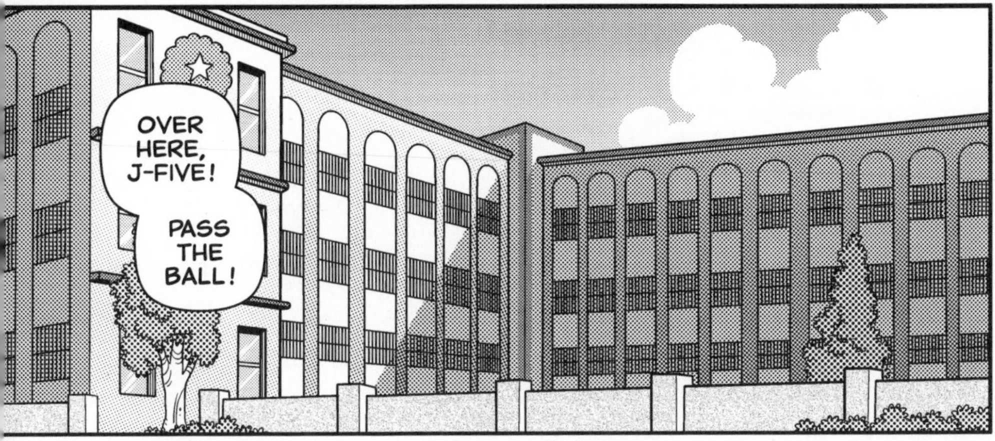
OVER HERE, J-FIVE!
PASS THE BALL!
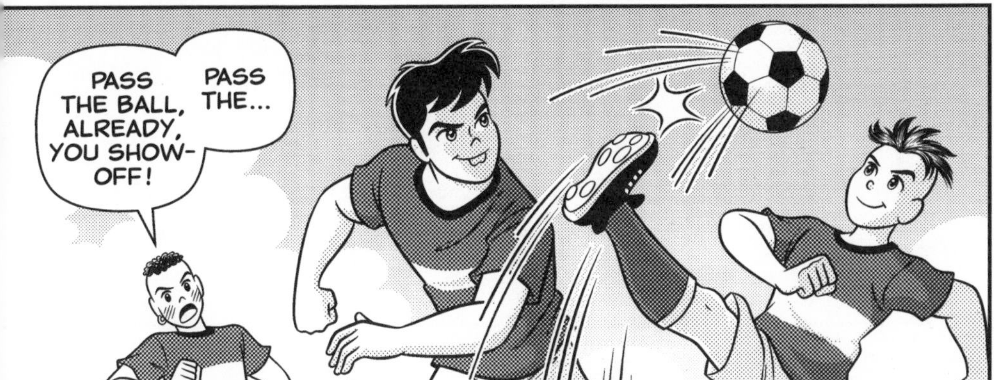
PASS THE BALL, ALREADY, YOU SHOW-OFF!
PASS THE...
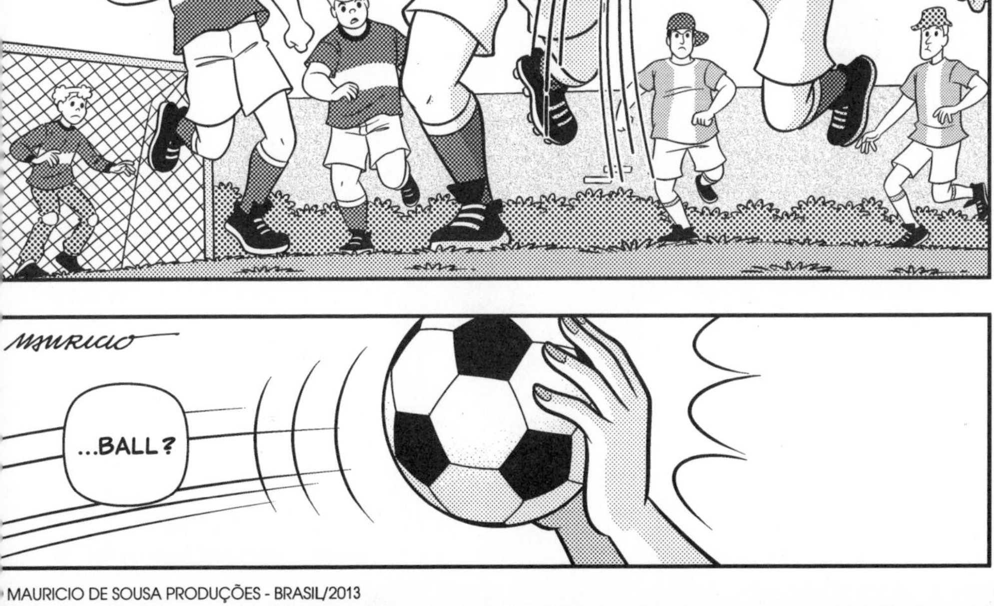
MAURICIO
...BALL?

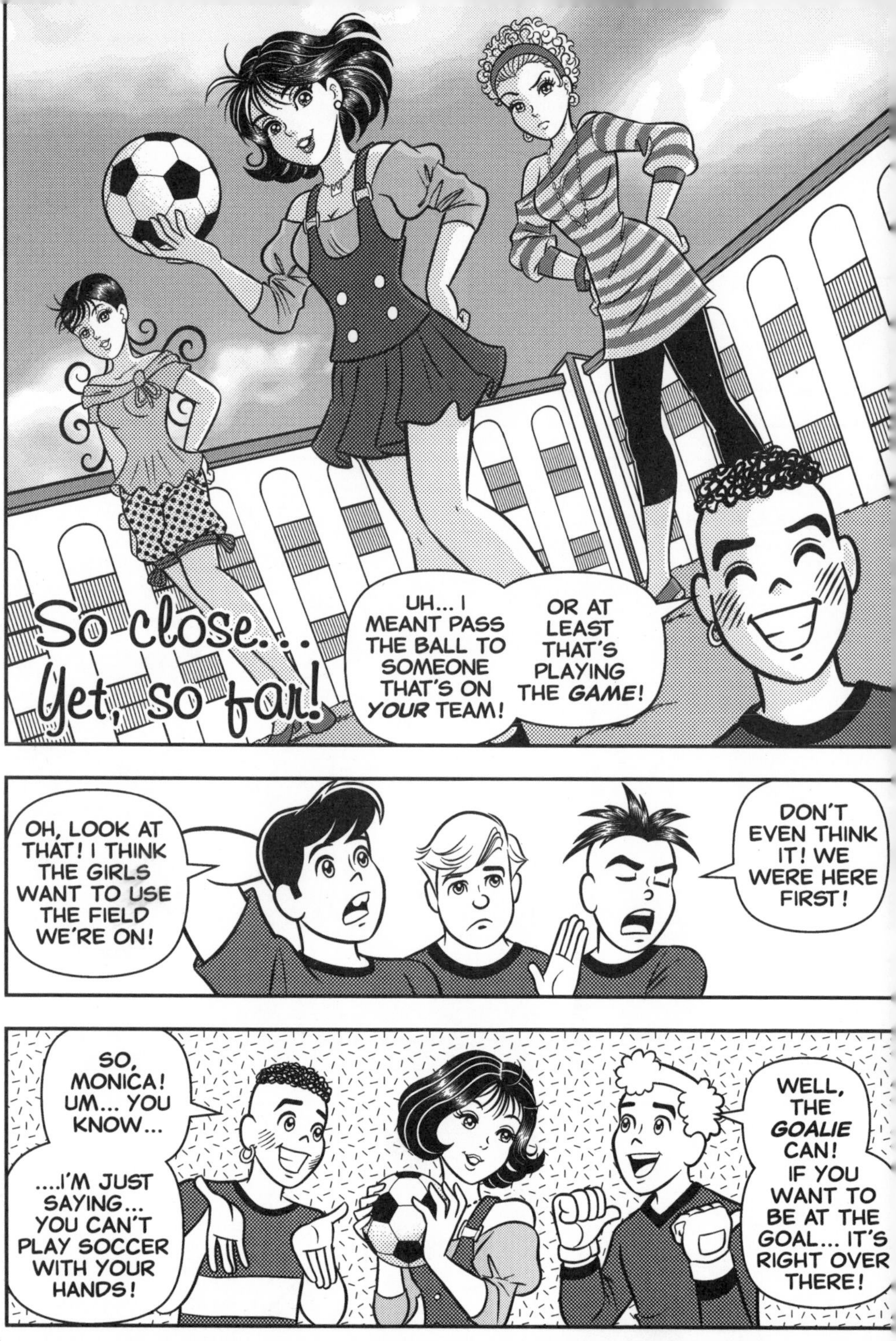
So close... Yet, so far!
UH... I MEANT PASS THE BALL TO SOMEONE THAT'S ON *YOUR* TEAM!
OR AT LEAST THAT'S PLAYING THE *GAME*!
OH, LOOK AT THAT! I THINK THE GIRLS WANT TO USE THE FIELD WE'RE ON!
DON'T EVEN THINK IT! WE WERE HERE FIRST!
SO, MONICA! UM... YOU KNOW...
....I'M JUST SAYING... YOU CAN'T PLAY SOCCER WITH YOUR HANDS!
WELL, THE *GOALIE* CAN! IF YOU WANT TO BE AT THE GOAL... IT'S RIGHT OVER THERE!

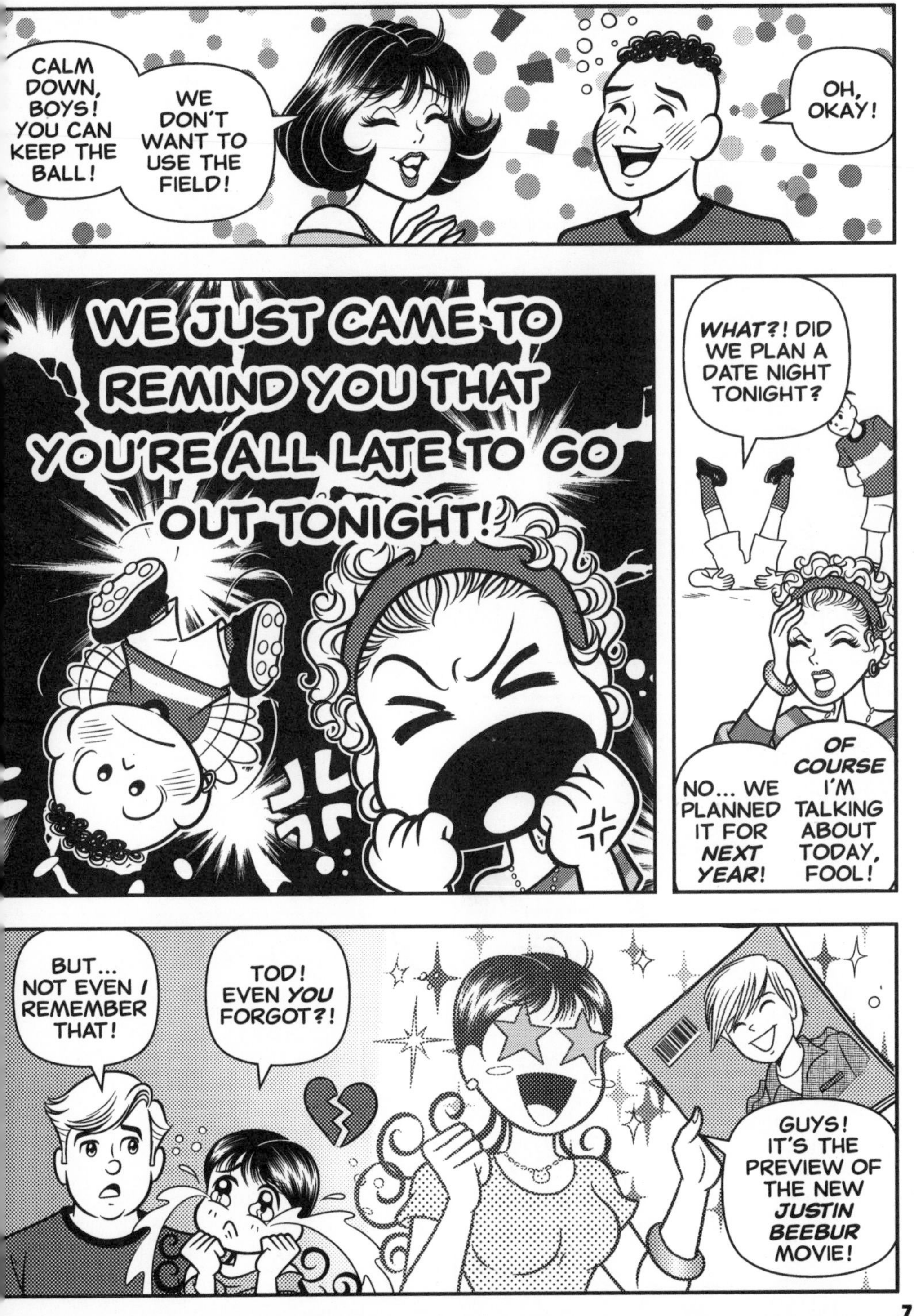
CALM DOWN, BOYS! YOU CAN KEEP THE BALL!
WE DON'T WANT TO USE THE FIELD!
OH, OKAY!
WE JUST CAME TO REMIND YOU THAT YOU'RE ALL LATE TO GO OUT TONIGHT!
WHAT?! DID WE PLAN A DATE NIGHT TONIGHT?
NO... WE PLANNED IT FOR NEXT YEAR!
OF COURSE I'M TALKING ABOUT TODAY, FOOL!
BUT... NOT EVEN I REMEMBER THAT!
TOD! EVEN YOU FORGOT?!
GUYS! IT'S THE PREVIEW OF THE NEW JUSTIN BEEBUR MOVIE!

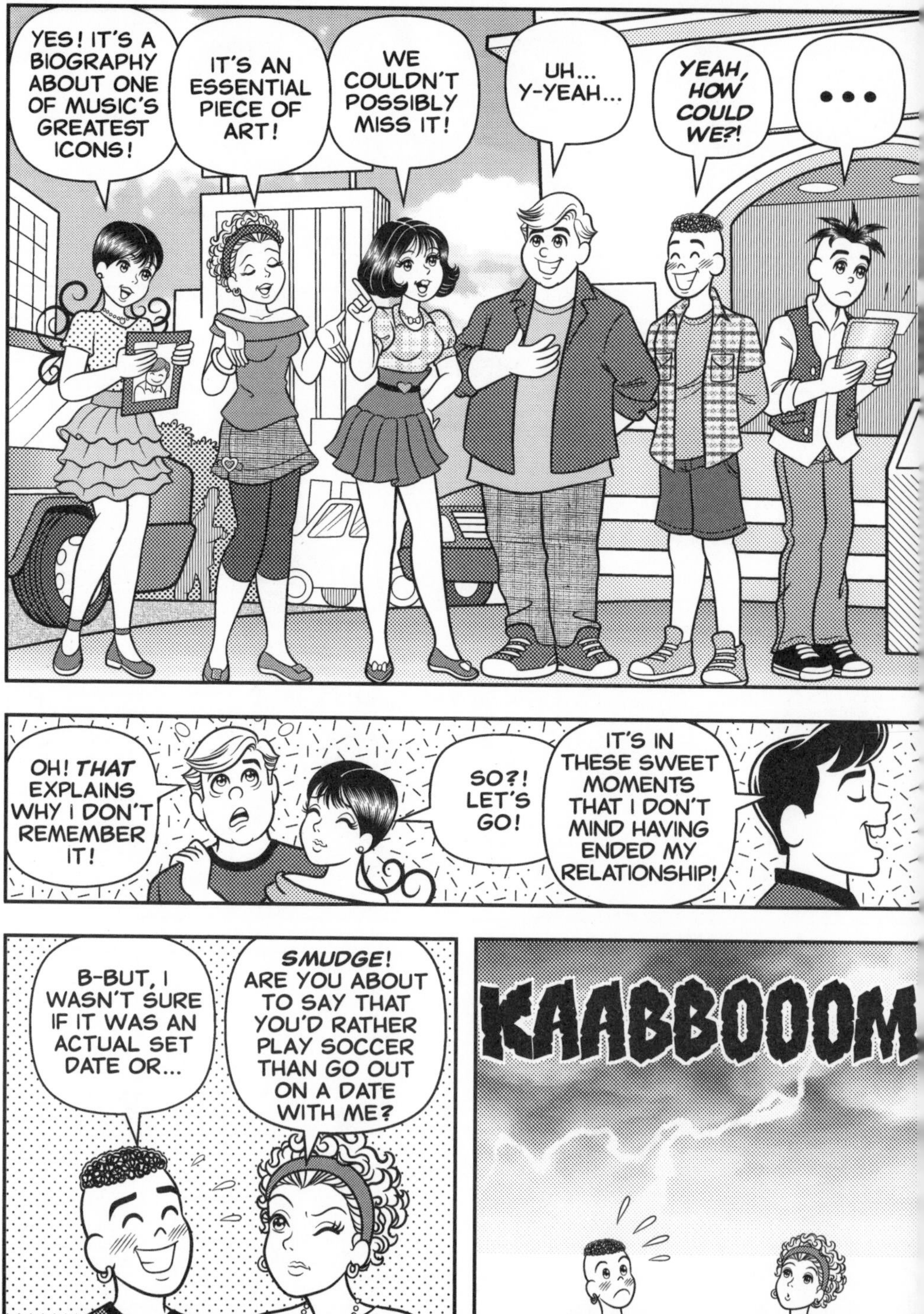
YES! IT'S A BIOGRAPHY ABOUT ONE OF MUSIC'S GREATEST ICONS!
IT'S AN ESSENTIAL PIECE OF ART!
WE COULDN'T POSSIBLY MISS IT!
UH... Y-YEAH...
YEAH, HOW COULD WE?!
...
OH! *THAT* EXPLAINS WHY I DON'T REMEMBER IT!
SO?! LET'S GO!
IT'S IN THESE SWEET MOMENTS THAT I DON'T MIND HAVING ENDED MY RELATIONSHIP!
B-BUT, I WASN'T SURE IF IT WAS AN ACTUAL SET DATE OR...
SMUDGE! ARE YOU ABOUT TO SAY THAT YOU'D RATHER PLAY SOCCER THAN GO OUT ON A DATE WITH ME?
KAABBOOOM

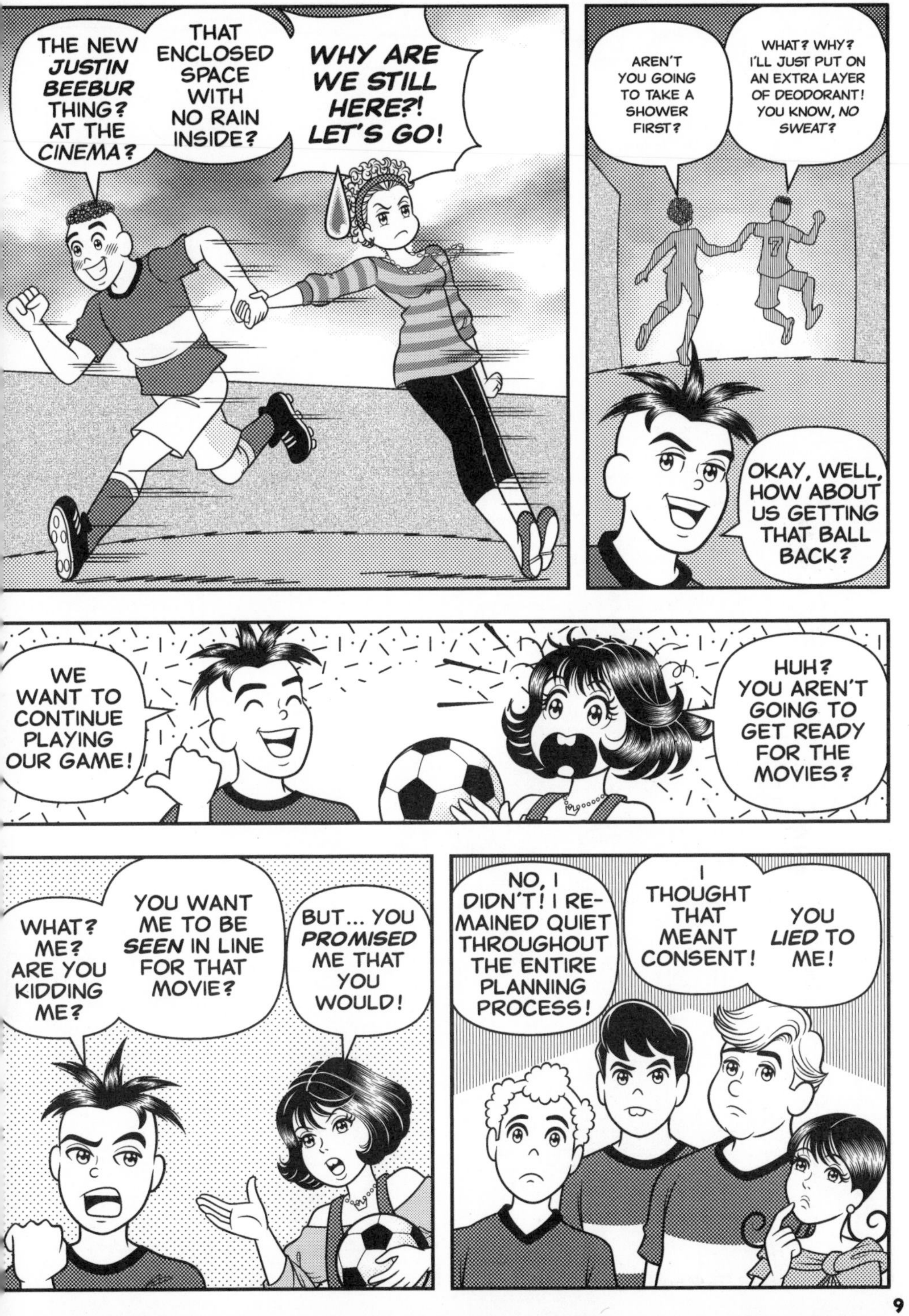
THE NEW JUSTIN BEEBUR THING? AT THE CINEMA?
THAT ENCLOSED SPACE WITH NO RAIN INSIDE?
WHY ARE WE STILL HERE?! LET'S GO!
AREN'T YOU GOING TO TAKE A SHOWER FIRST?
WHAT? WHY? I'LL JUST PUT ON AN EXTRA LAYER OF DEODORANT! YOU KNOW, NO SWEAT?
7
OKAY, WELL, HOW ABOUT US GETTING THAT BALL BACK?
WE WANT TO CONTINUE PLAYING OUR GAME!
HUH? YOU AREN'T GOING TO GET READY FOR THE MOVIES?
WHAT? ME? ARE YOU KIDDING ME?
YOU WANT ME TO BE SEEN IN LINE FOR THAT MOVIE?
BUT... YOU PROMISED ME THAT YOU WOULD!
NO, I DIDN'T! I RE-MAINED QUIET THROUGHOUT THE ENTIRE PLANNING PROCESS!
I THOUGHT THAT MEANT CONSENT!
YOU LIED TO ME!

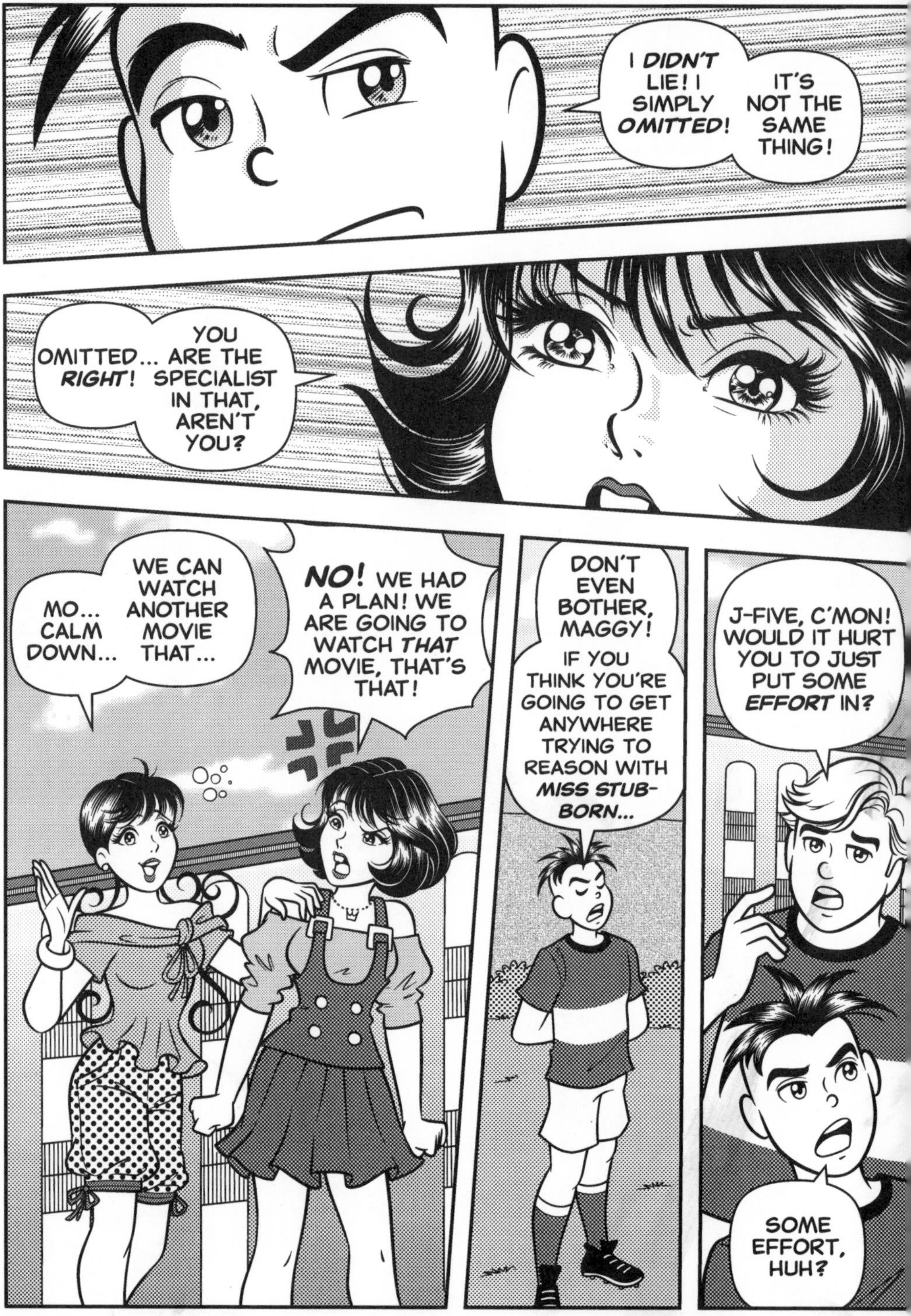
I DIDN'T LIE! I SIMPLY OMITTED!
IT'S NOT THE SAME THING!
OMITTED... RIGHT!
YOU ARE THE SPECIALIST IN THAT, AREN'T YOU?
MO... CALM DOWN...
WE CAN WATCH ANOTHER MOVIE THAT...
NO! WE HAD A PLAN! WE ARE GOING TO WATCH THAT MOVIE, THAT'S THAT!
DON'T EVEN BOTHER, MAGGY!
IF YOU THINK YOU'RE GOING TO GET ANYWHERE TRYING TO REASON WITH MISS STUB-BORN...
J-FIVE, C'MON! WOULD IT HURT YOU TO JUST PUT SOME EFFORT IN?
SOME EFFORT, HUH?

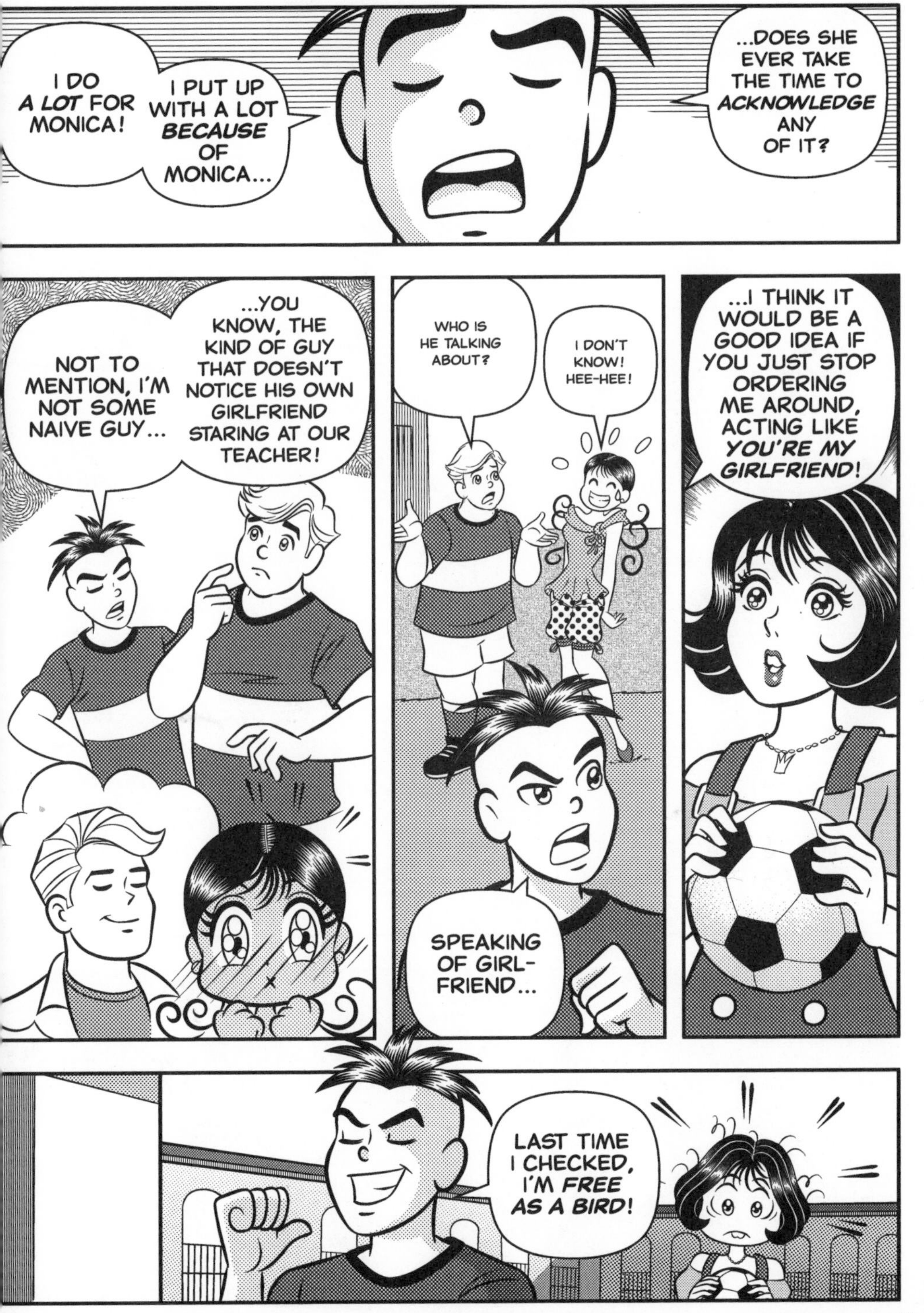
I DO A *LOT* FOR MONICA!
I PUT UP WITH A LOT *BECAUSE* OF MONICA...
...DOES SHE EVER TAKE THE TIME TO *ACKNOWLEDGE* ANY OF IT?
NOT TO MENTION, I'M NOT SOME NAIVE GUY...
...YOU KNOW, THE KIND OF GUY THAT DOESN'T NOTICE HIS OWN GIRLFRIEND STARING AT OUR TEACHER!
WHO IS HE TALKING ABOUT?
I DON'T KNOW! HEE-HEE!
SPEAKING OF GIRL-FRIEND...
...I THINK IT WOULD BE A GOOD IDEA IF YOU JUST STOP ORDERING ME AROUND, ACTING LIKE *YOU'RE MY GIRLFRIEND*!
LAST TIME I CHECKED, I'M *FREE AS A BIRD*!

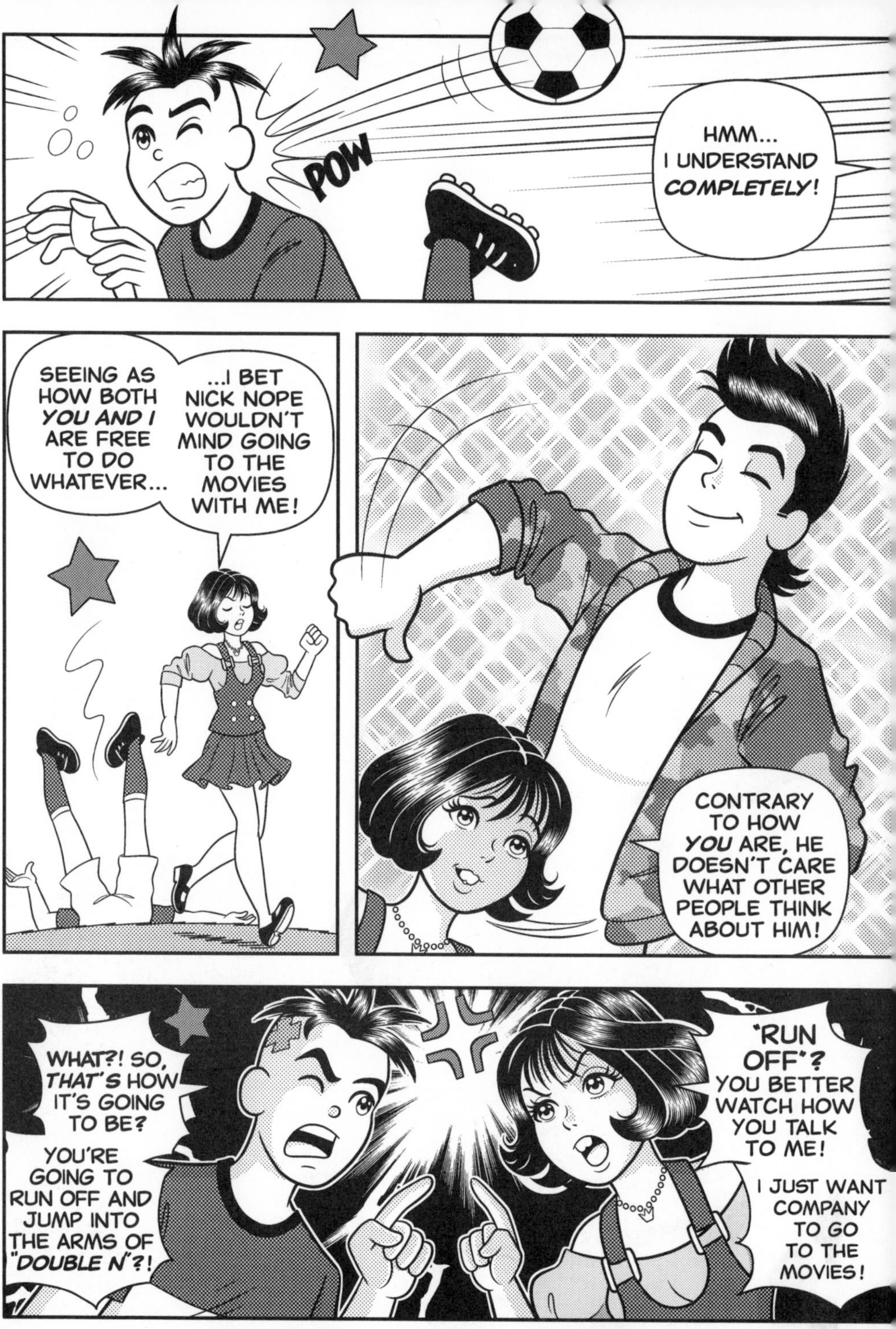
POW
HMM... I UNDERSTAND COMPLETELY!
SEEING AS HOW BOTH YOU AND I ARE FREE TO DO WHATEVER...
...I BET NICK NOPE WOULDN'T MIND GOING TO THE MOVIES WITH ME!
CONTRARY TO HOW YOU ARE, HE DOESN'T CARE WHAT OTHER PEOPLE THINK ABOUT HIM!
WHAT?! SO, THAT'S HOW IT'S GOING TO BE?
YOU'RE GOING TO RUN OFF AND JUMP INTO THE ARMS OF "DOUBLE N"?!
"RUN OFF"? YOU BETTER WATCH HOW YOU TALK TO ME!
I JUST WANT COMPANY TO GO TO THE MOVIES!

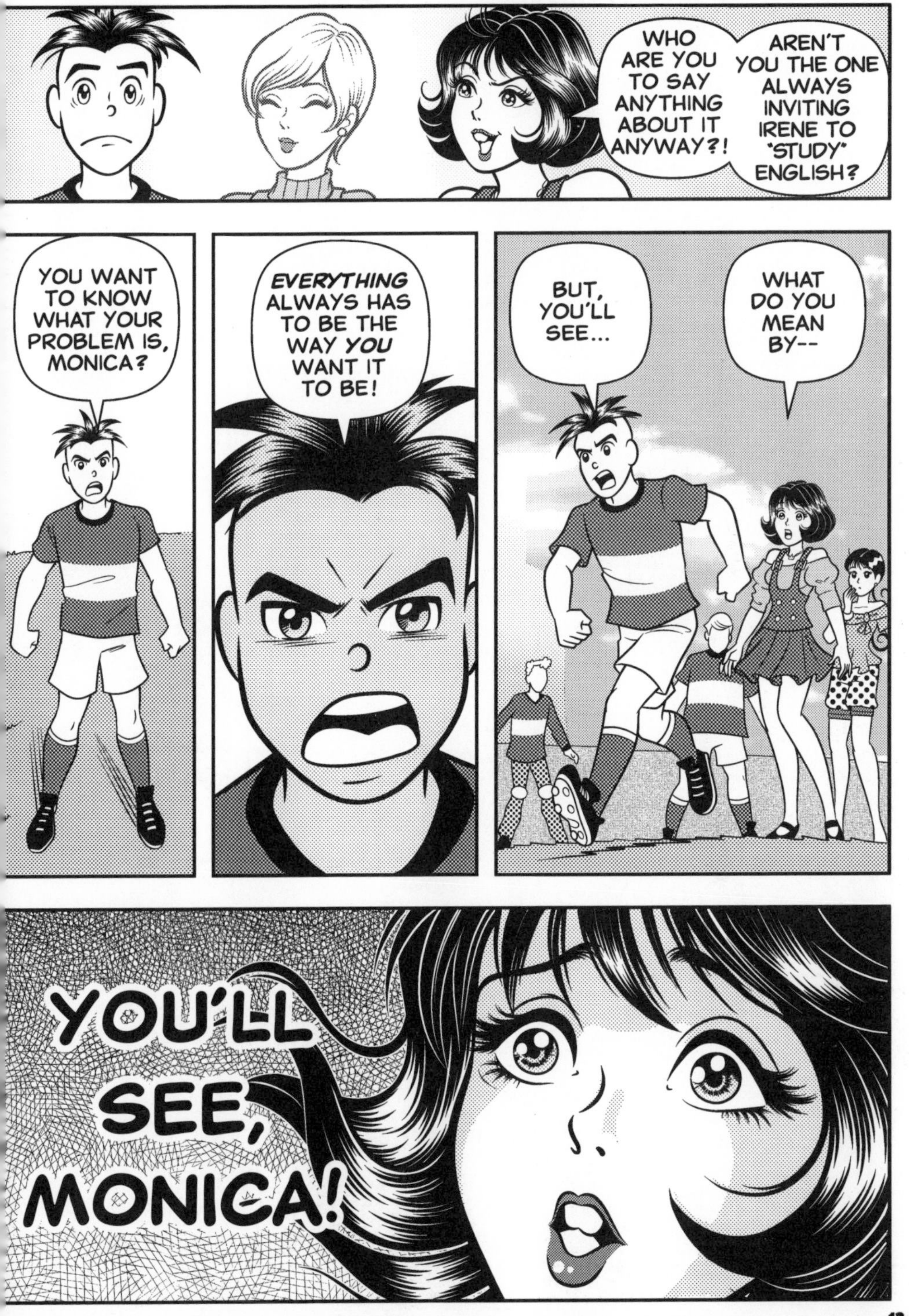
WHO ARE YOU TO SAY ANYTHING ABOUT IT ANYWAY?!
AREN'T YOU THE ONE ALWAYS INVITING IRENE TO "STUDY" ENGLISH?
YOU WANT TO KNOW WHAT YOUR PROBLEM IS, MONICA?
EVERYTHING ALWAYS HAS TO BE THE WAY *YOU* WANT IT TO BE!
BUT, YOU'LL SEE...
WHAT DO YOU MEAN BY--
YOU'LL SEE, MONICA!

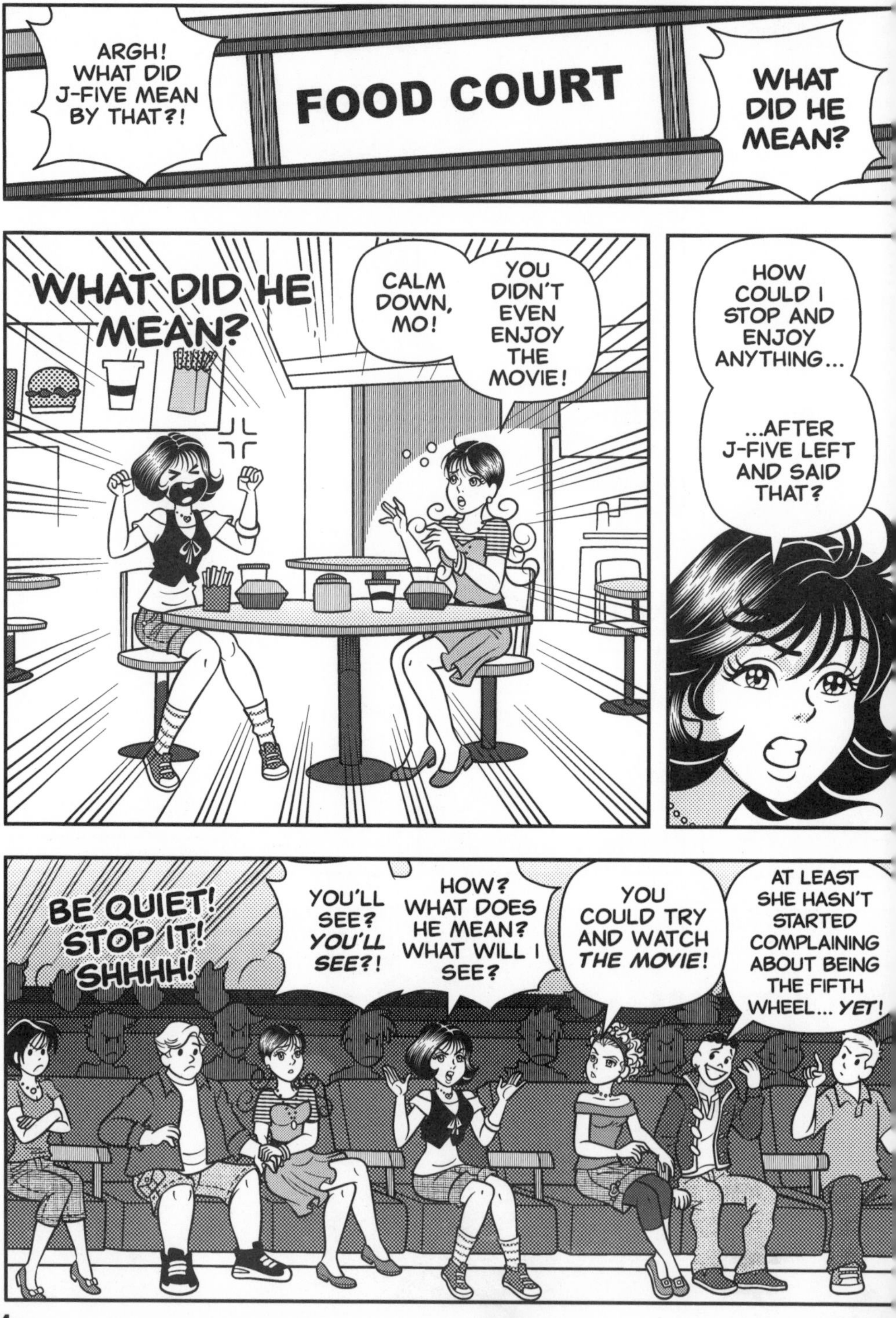
ARGH! WHAT DID J-FIVE MEAN BY THAT?!
FOOD COURT
WHAT DID HE MEAN?
WHAT DID HE MEAN?
CALM DOWN, MO!
YOU DIDN'T EVEN ENJOY THE MOVIE!
HOW COULD I STOP AND ENJOY ANYTHING...
...AFTER J-FIVE LEFT AND SAID THAT?
BE QUIET! STOP IT! SHHHH!
YOU'LL SEE? *YOU'LL SEE?!*
HOW? WHAT DOES HE MEAN? WHAT WILL I SEE?
YOU COULD TRY AND WATCH *THE MOVIE*!
AT LEAST SHE HASN'T STARTED COMPLAINING ABOUT BEING THE FIFTH WHEEL... *YET*!

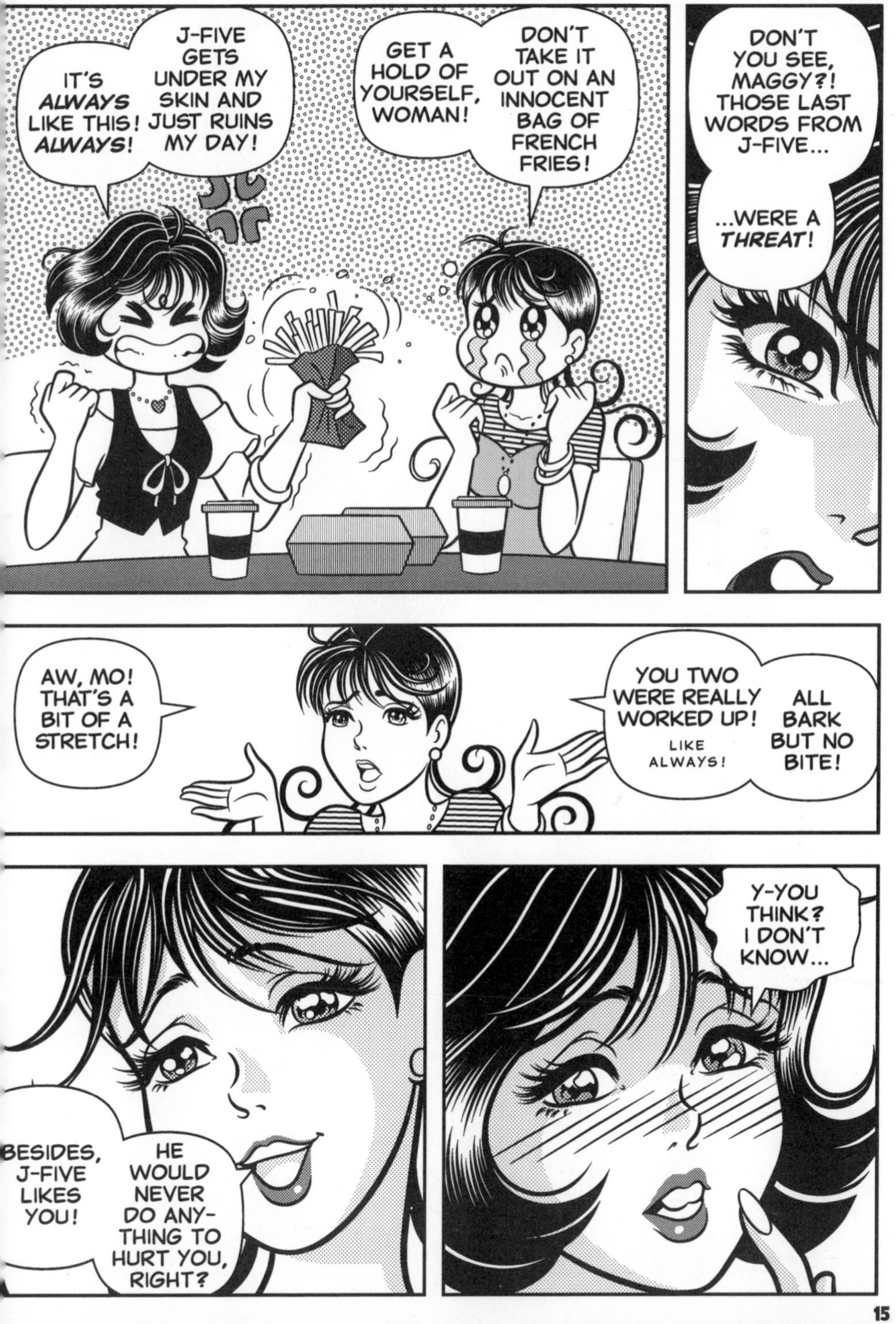
IT'S *ALWAYS* LIKE THIS! *ALWAYS*!
J-FIVE GETS UNDER MY SKIN AND JUST RUINS MY DAY!
GET A HOLD OF YOURSELF, WOMAN!
DON'T TAKE IT OUT ON AN INNOCENT BAG OF FRENCH FRIES!
DON'T YOU SEE, MAGGY?! THOSE LAST WORDS FROM J-FIVE...
...WERE A *THREAT*!
AW, MO! THAT'S A BIT OF A STRETCH!
YOU TWO WERE REALLY WORKED UP!
LIKE ALWAYS!
ALL BARK BUT NO BITE!
BESIDES, J-FIVE LIKES YOU!
HE WOULD NEVER DO ANY-THING TO HURT YOU, RIGHT?
Y-YOU THINK? I DON'T KNOW...

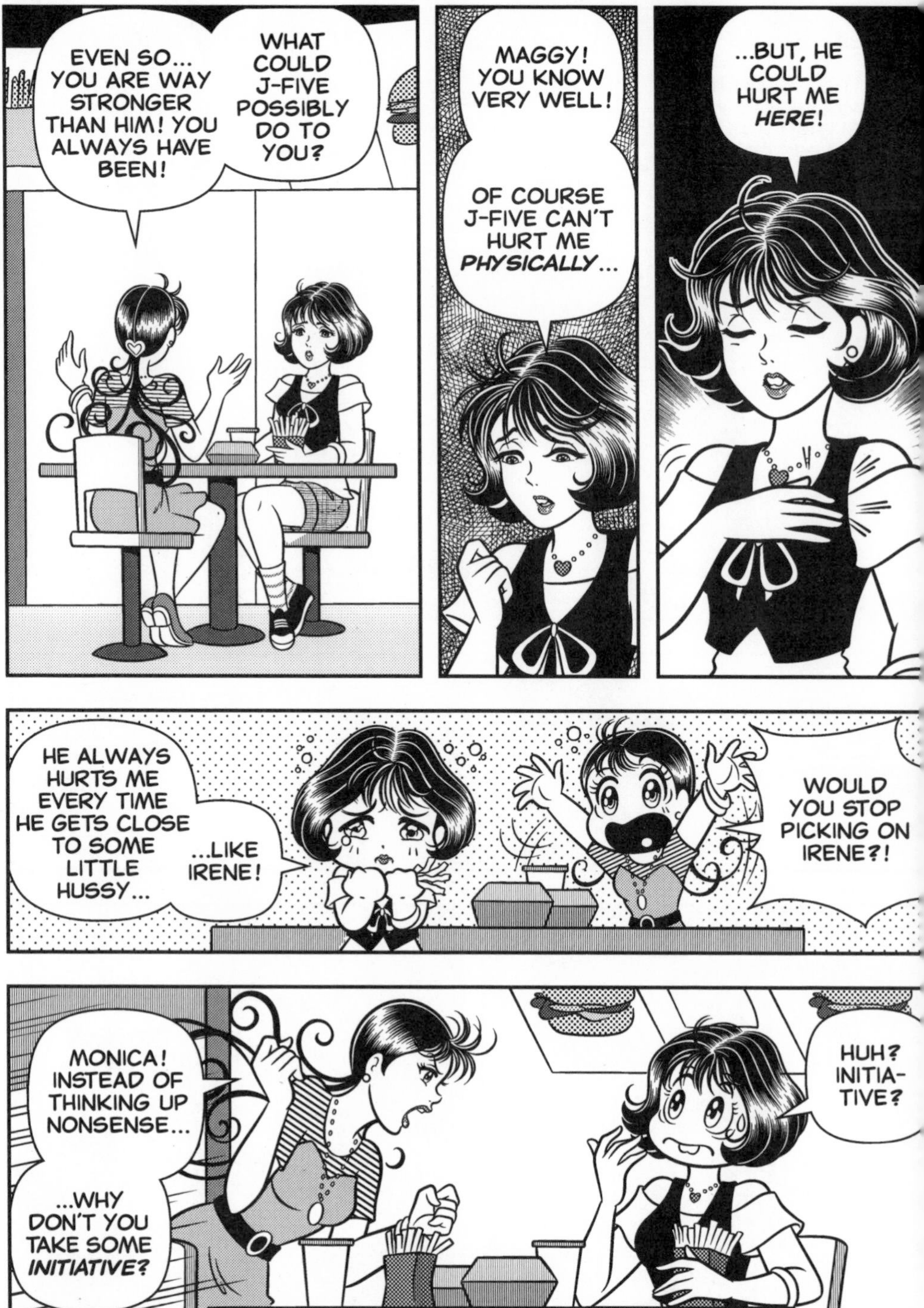
EVEN SO... YOU ARE WAY STRONGER THAN HIM! YOU ALWAYS HAVE BEEN!
WHAT COULD J-FIVE POSSIBLY DO TO YOU?
MAGGY! YOU KNOW VERY WELL!
OF COURSE J-FIVE CAN'T HURT ME PHYSICALLY...
...BUT, HE COULD HURT ME HERE!
HE ALWAYS HURTS ME EVERY TIME HE GETS CLOSE TO SOME LITTLE HUSSY...
...LIKE IRENE!
WOULD YOU STOP PICKING ON IRENE?!
MONICA! INSTEAD OF THINKING UP NONSENSE...
...WHY DON'T YOU TAKE SOME INITIATIVE?
HUH? INITIA-TIVE?

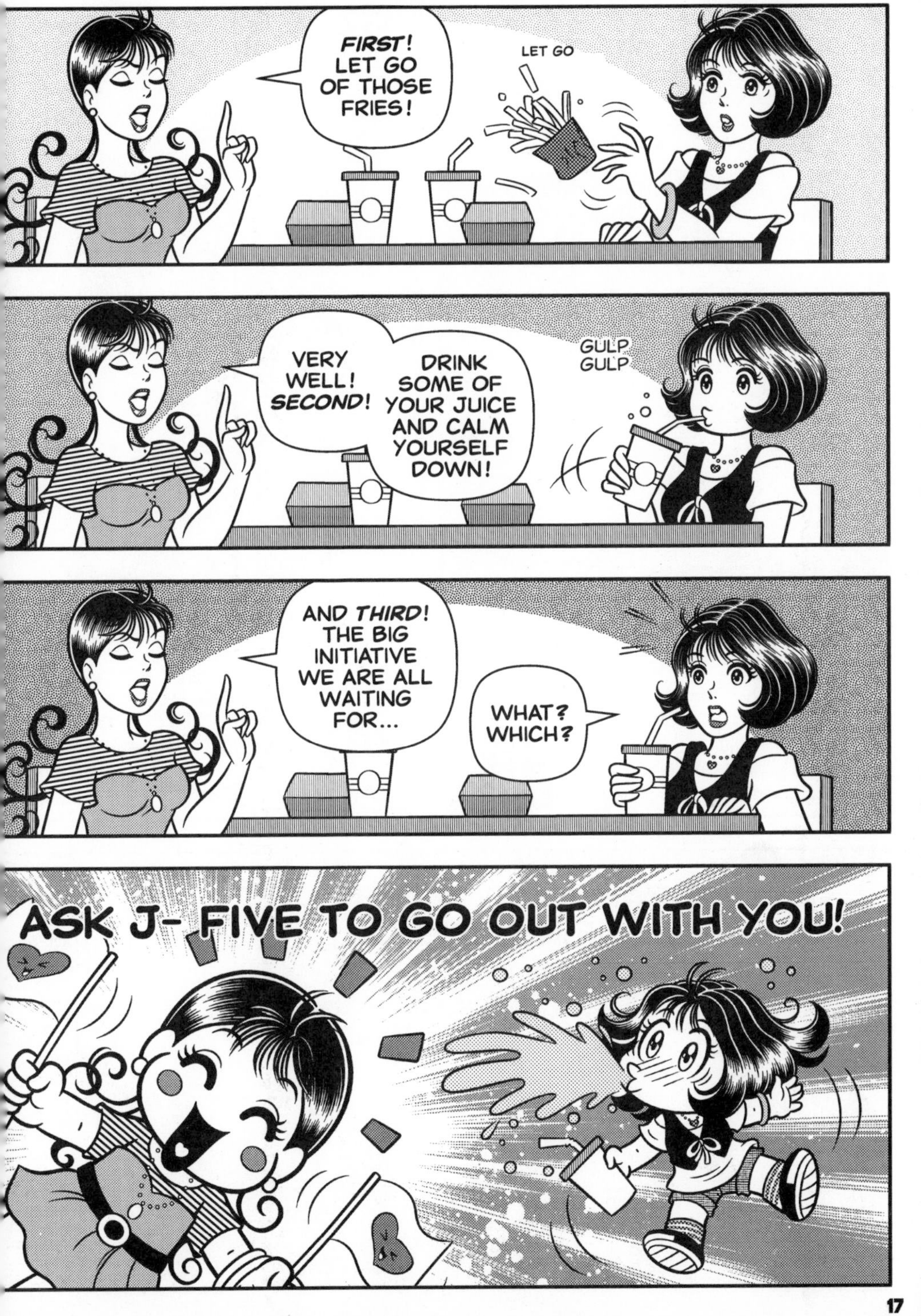
FIRST! LET GO OF THOSE FRIES!
LET GO
VERY WELL! SECOND!
DRINK SOME OF YOUR JUICE AND CALM YOURSELF DOWN!
GULP GULP
AND THIRD! THE BIG INITIATIVE WE ARE ALL WAITING FOR...
WHAT? WHICH?
ASK J-FIVE TO GO OUT WITH YOU!

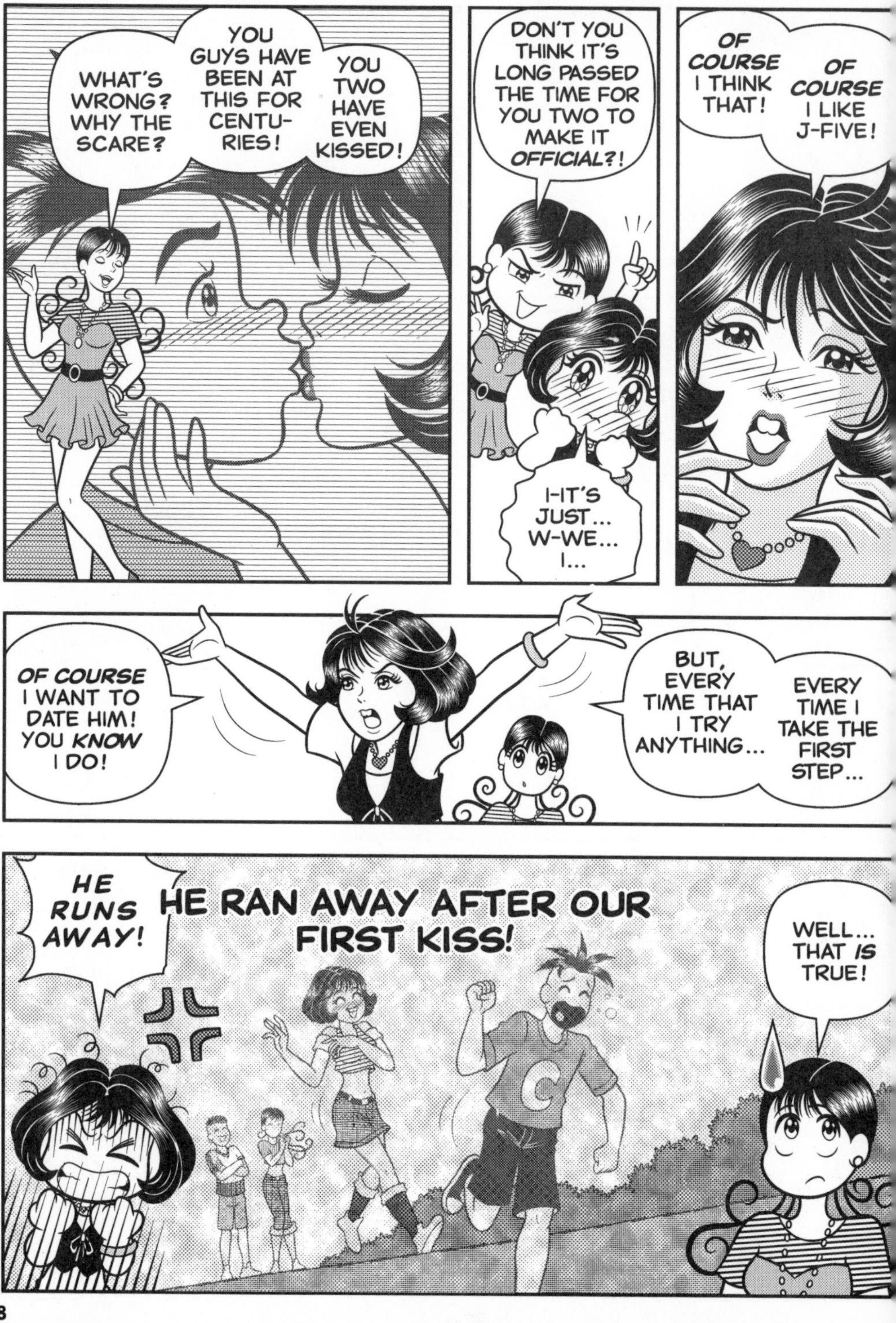
WHAT'S WRONG? WHY THE SCARE?
YOU GUYS HAVE BEEN AT THIS FOR CENTU-RIES!
YOU TWO HAVE EVEN KISSED!
DON'T YOU THINK IT'S LONG PASSED THE TIME FOR YOU TWO TO MAKE IT *OFFICIAL?*!
I-IT'S JUST... W-WE... I...
OF COURSE I THINK THAT!
OF COURSE I LIKE J-FIVE!
OF COURSE I WANT TO DATE HIM! YOU *KNOW* I DO!
BUT, EVERY TIME THAT I TRY ANYTHING...
EVERY TIME I TAKE THE FIRST STEP...
HE RUNS AWAY!
HE RAN AWAY AFTER OUR FIRST KISS!
WELL... THAT *IS* TRUE!

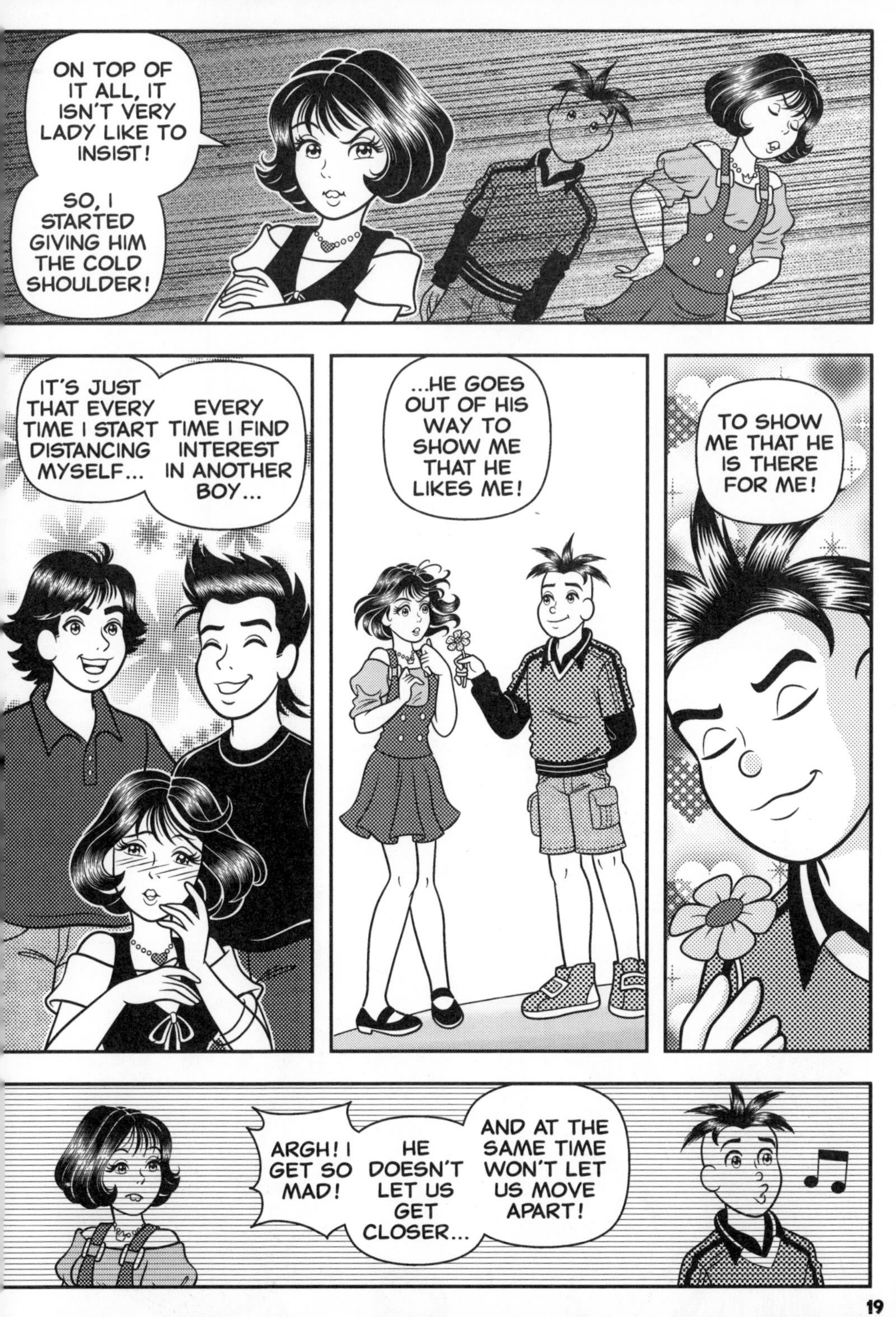
ON TOP OF IT ALL, IT ISN'T VERY LADY LIKE TO INSIST!
SO, I STARTED GIVING HIM THE COLD SHOULDER!
IT'S JUST THAT EVERY TIME I START DISTANCING MYSELF...
EVERY TIME I FIND INTEREST IN ANOTHER BOY...
...HE GOES OUT OF HIS WAY TO SHOW ME THAT HE LIKES ME!
TO SHOW ME THAT HE IS THERE FOR ME!
ARGH! I GET SO MAD!
HE DOESN'T LET US GET CLOSER...
AND AT THE SAME TIME WON'T LET US MOVE APART!

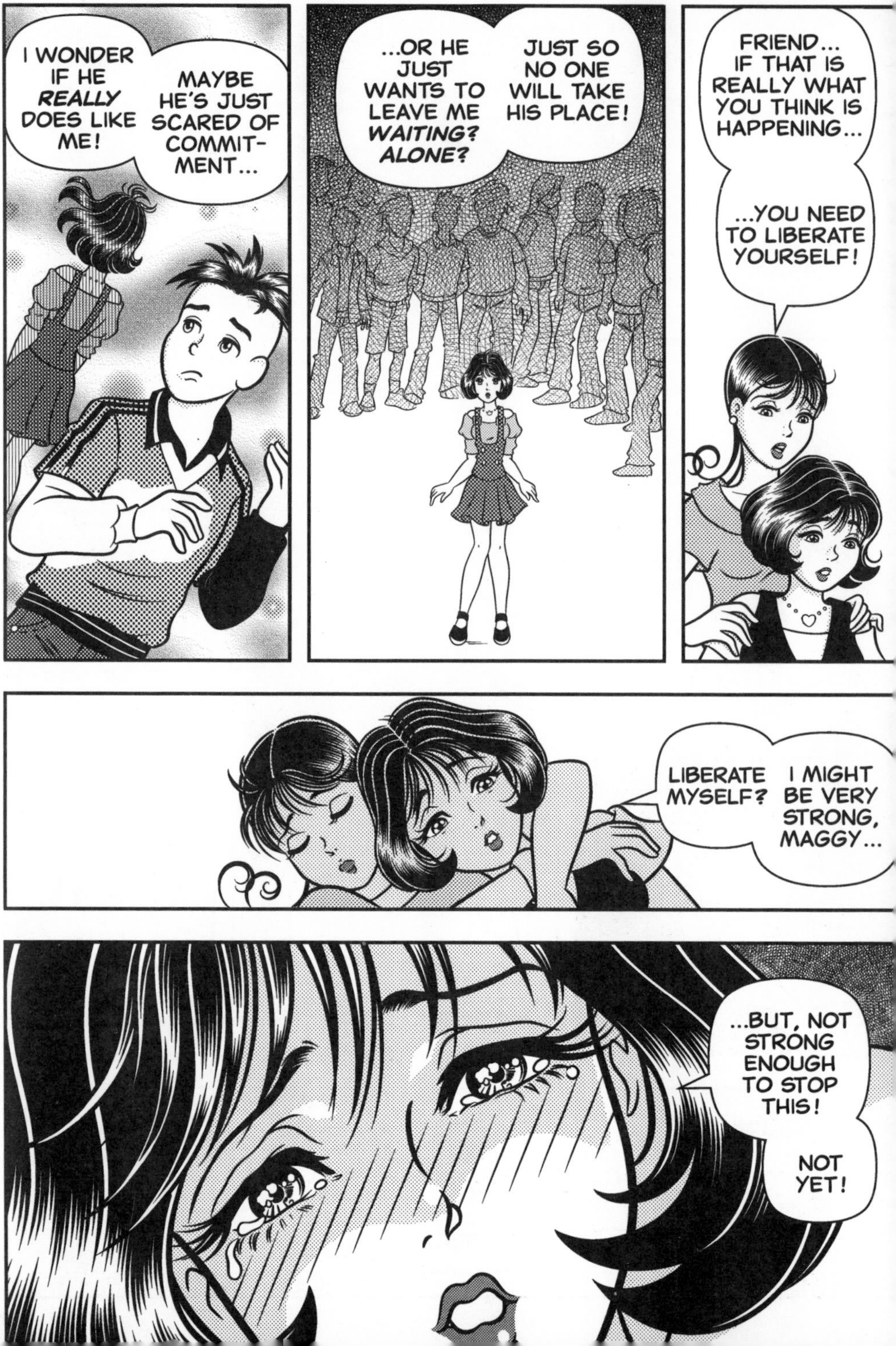
I WONDER IF HE *REALLY* DOES LIKE ME!
MAYBE HE'S JUST SCARED OF COMMIT-MENT...
...OR HE JUST WANTS TO LEAVE ME *WAITING? ALONE?*
JUST SO NO ONE WILL TAKE HIS PLACE!
FRIEND... IF THAT IS REALLY WHAT YOU THINK IS HAPPENING...
...YOU NEED TO LIBERATE YOURSELF!
LIBERATE MYSELF?
I MIGHT BE VERY STRONG, MAGGY...
...BUT, NOT STRONG ENOUGH TO STOP THIS!
NOT YET!

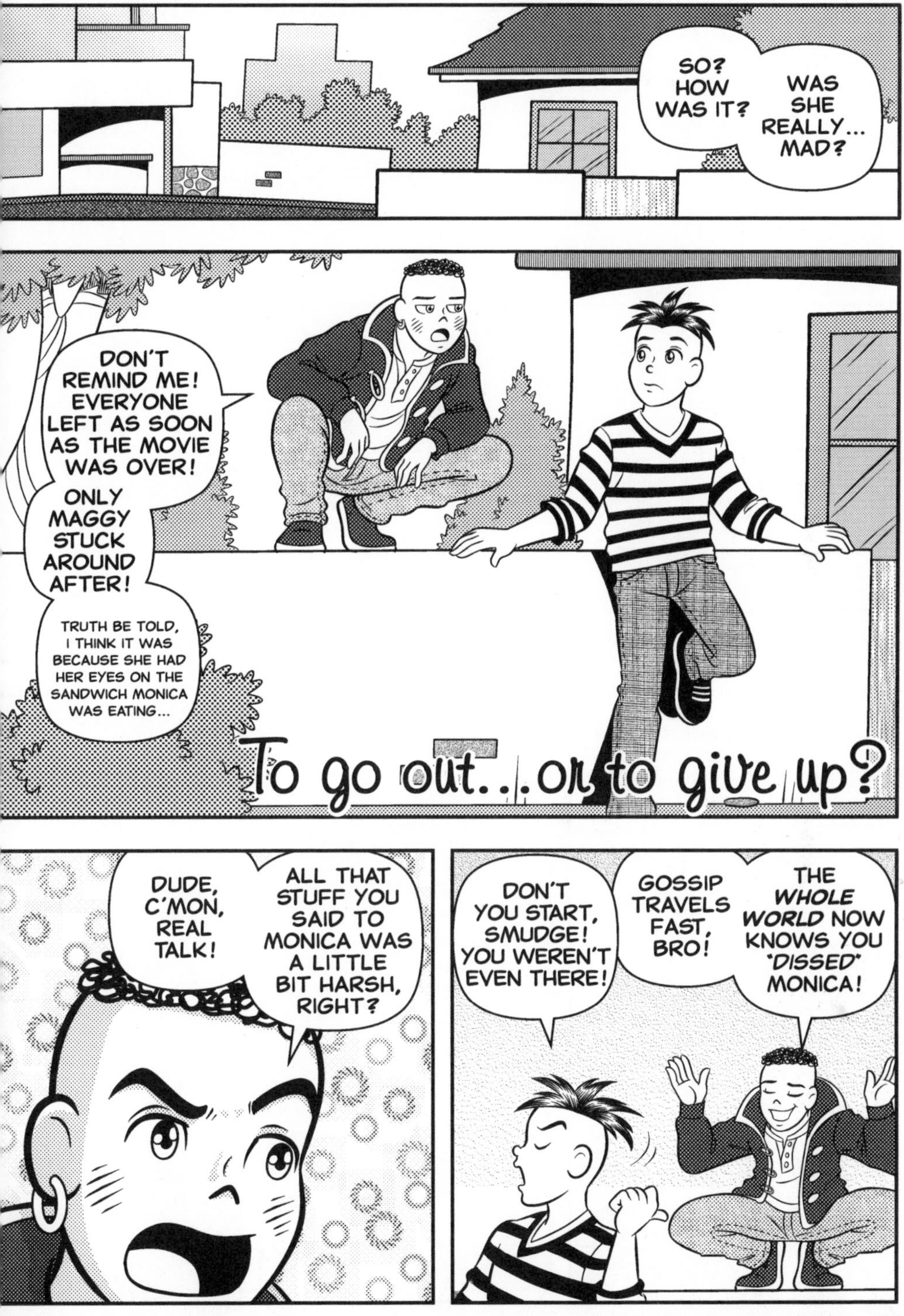
SO? HOW WAS IT?
WAS SHE REALLY... MAD?
DON'T REMIND ME! EVERYONE LEFT AS SOON AS THE MOVIE WAS OVER!
ONLY MAGGY STUCK AROUND AFTER!
TRUTH BE TOLD, I THINK IT WAS BECAUSE SHE HAD HER EYES ON THE SANDWICH MONICA WAS EATING...
To go out... or to give up?
DUDE, C'MON, REAL TALK!
ALL THAT STUFF YOU SAID TO MONICA WAS A LITTLE BIT HARSH, RIGHT?
DON'T YOU START, SMUDGE! YOU WEREN'T EVEN THERE!
GOSSIP TRAVELS FAST, BRO!
THE *WHOLE WORLD* NOW KNOWS YOU *"DISSED"* MONICA!

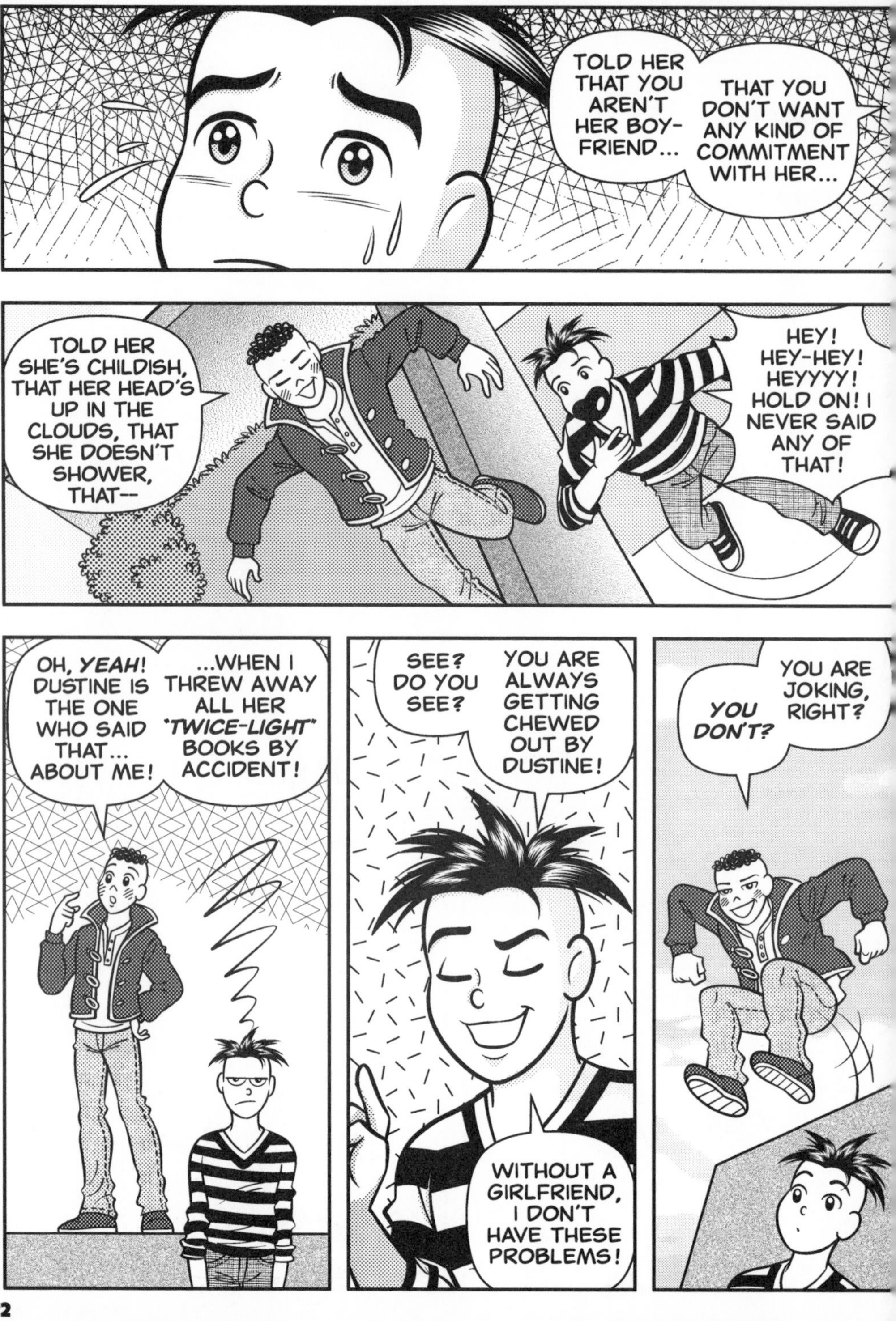
TOLD HER THAT YOU AREN'T HER BOY-FRIEND...
THAT YOU DON'T WANT ANY KIND OF COMMITMENT WITH HER...
TOLD HER SHE'S CHILDISH, THAT HER HEAD'S UP IN THE CLOUDS, THAT SHE DOESN'T SHOWER, THAT--
HEY! HEY-HEY! HEYYYY! HOLD ON! I NEVER SAID ANY OF THAT!
OH, YEAH! DUSTINE IS THE ONE WHO SAID THAT... ABOUT ME!
...WHEN I THREW AWAY ALL HER "TWICE-LIGHT" BOOKS BY ACCIDENT!
SEE? DO YOU SEE?
YOU ARE ALWAYS GETTING CHEWED OUT BY DUSTINE!
WITHOUT A GIRLFRIEND, I DON'T HAVE THESE PROBLEMS!
YOU DON'T?
YOU ARE JOKING, RIGHT?

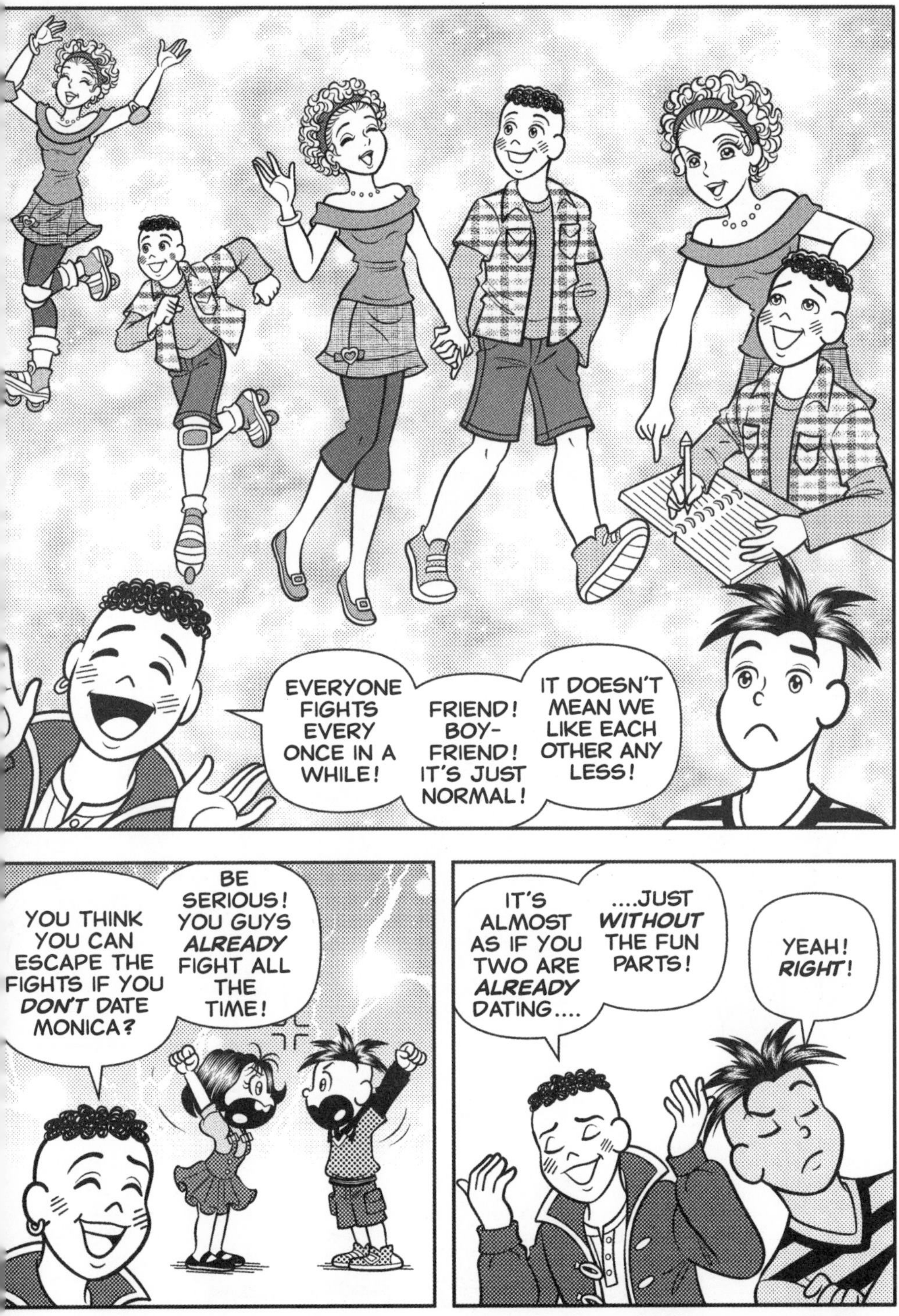
EVERYONE FIGHTS EVERY ONCE IN A WHILE!
FRIEND! BOY-FRIEND! IT'S JUST NORMAL!
IT DOESN'T MEAN WE LIKE EACH OTHER ANY LESS!
YOU THINK YOU CAN ESCAPE THE FIGHTS IF YOU *DON'T* DATE MONICA?
BE SERIOUS! YOU GUYS *ALREADY* FIGHT ALL THE TIME!
IT'S ALMOST AS IF YOU TWO ARE *ALREADY* DATING....
....JUST *WITHOUT* THE FUN PARTS!
YEAH! *RIGHT*!

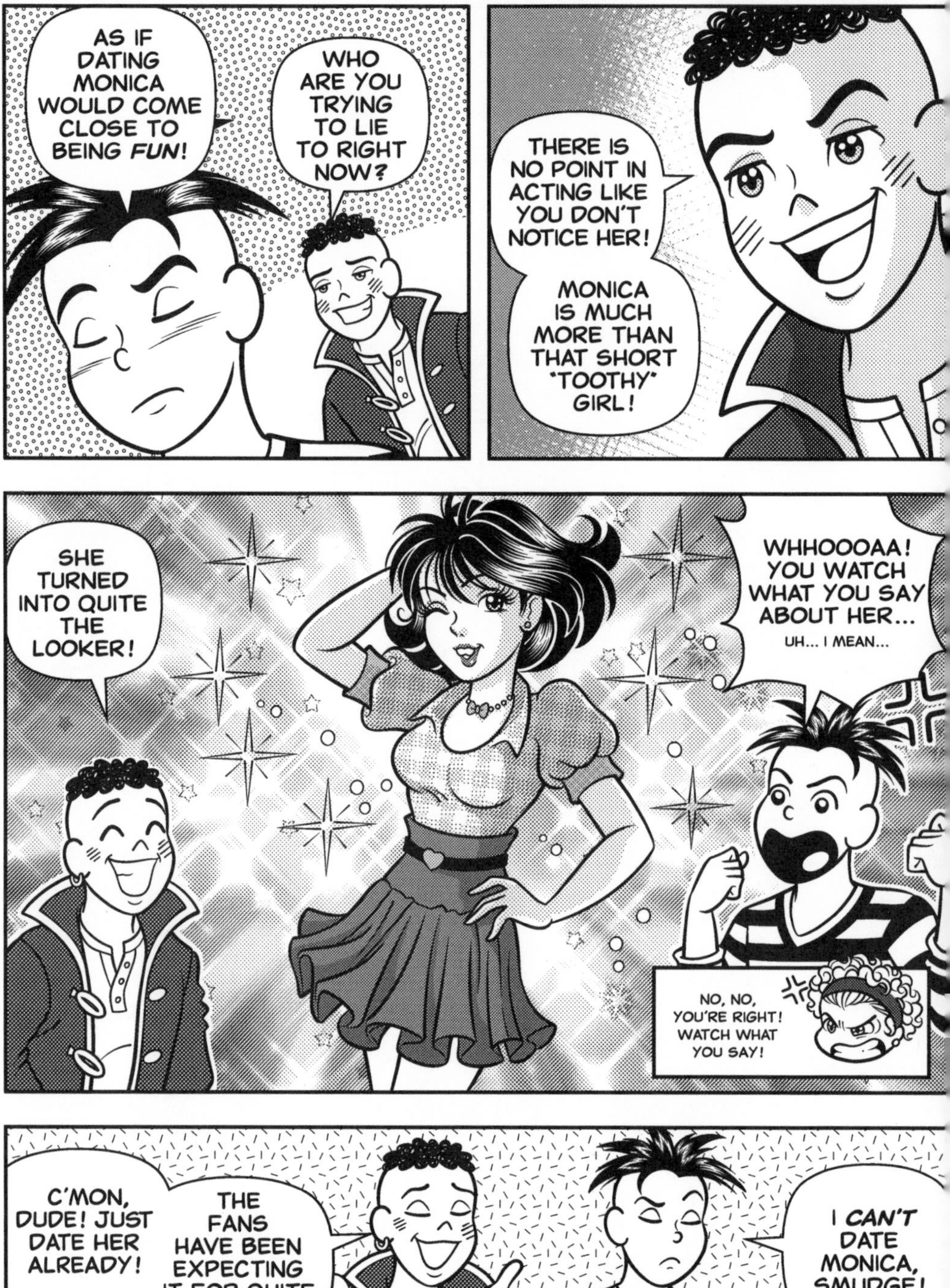
AS IF DATING MONICA WOULD COME CLOSE TO BEING *FUN*!
WHO ARE YOU TRYING TO LIE TO RIGHT NOW?
THERE IS NO POINT IN ACTING LIKE YOU DON'T NOTICE HER!
MONICA IS MUCH MORE THAN THAT SHORT "TOOTHY" GIRL!
SHE TURNED INTO QUITE THE LOOKER!
WHHOOOAA! YOU WATCH WHAT YOU SAY ABOUT HER...
UH... I MEAN...
NO, NO, YOU'RE RIGHT! WATCH WHAT YOU SAY!
C'MON, DUDE! JUST DATE HER ALREADY!
THE FANS HAVE BEEN EXPECTING IT FOR QUITE SOME TIME!
I *CAN'T* DATE MONICA, SMUDGE!

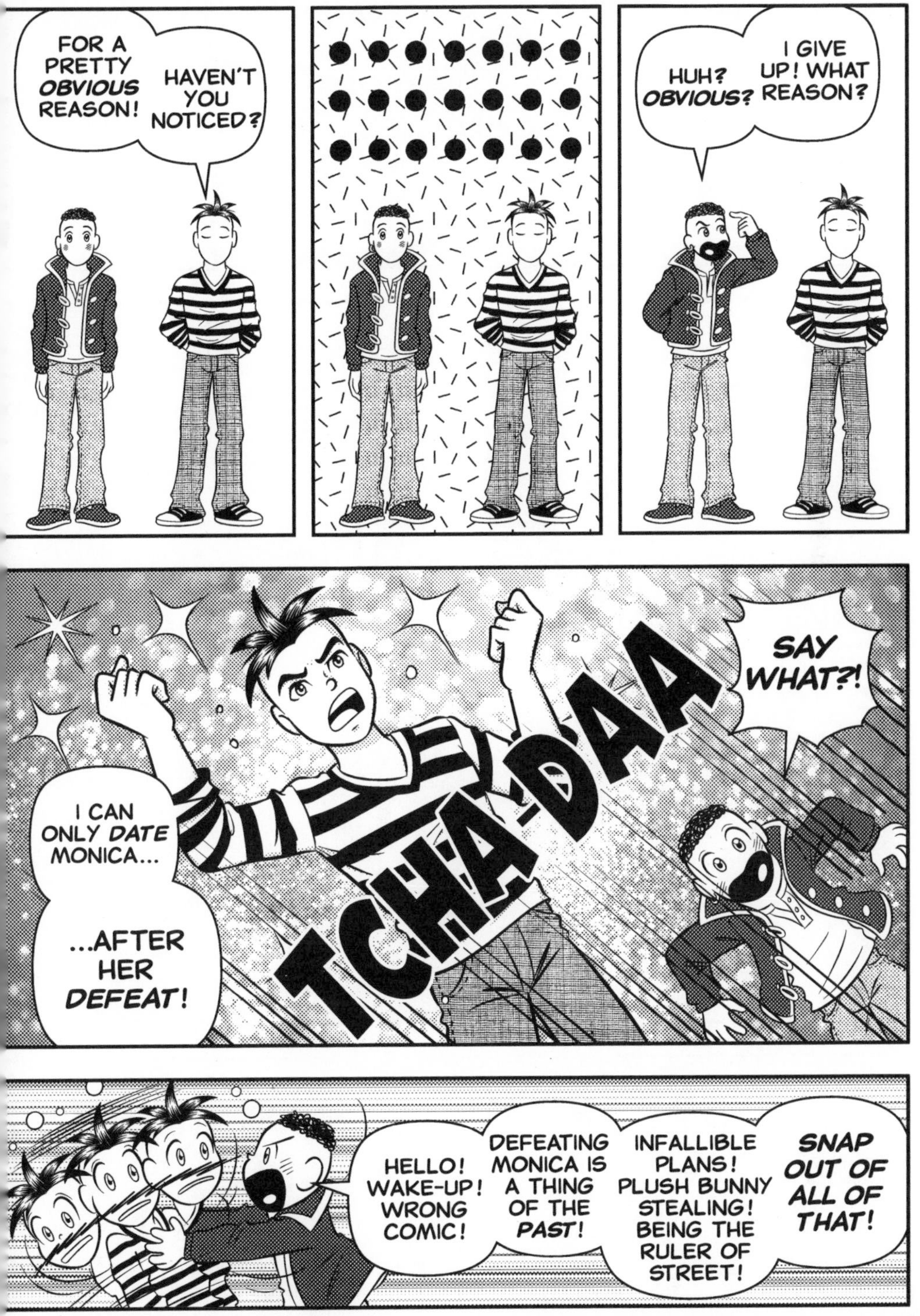
FOR A PRETTY OBVIOUS REASON!
HAVEN'T YOU NOTICED?
HUH? OBVIOUS?
I GIVE UP! WHAT REASON?
I CAN ONLY DATE MONICA...
...AFTER HER DEFEAT!
TCHA-DAA
SAY WHAT?!
HELLO! WAKE-UP! WRONG COMIC!
DEFEATING MONICA IS A THING OF THE PAST!
INFALLIBLE PLANS! PLUSH BUNNY STEALING! BEING THE RULER OF STREET!
SNAP OUT OF ALL OF THAT!

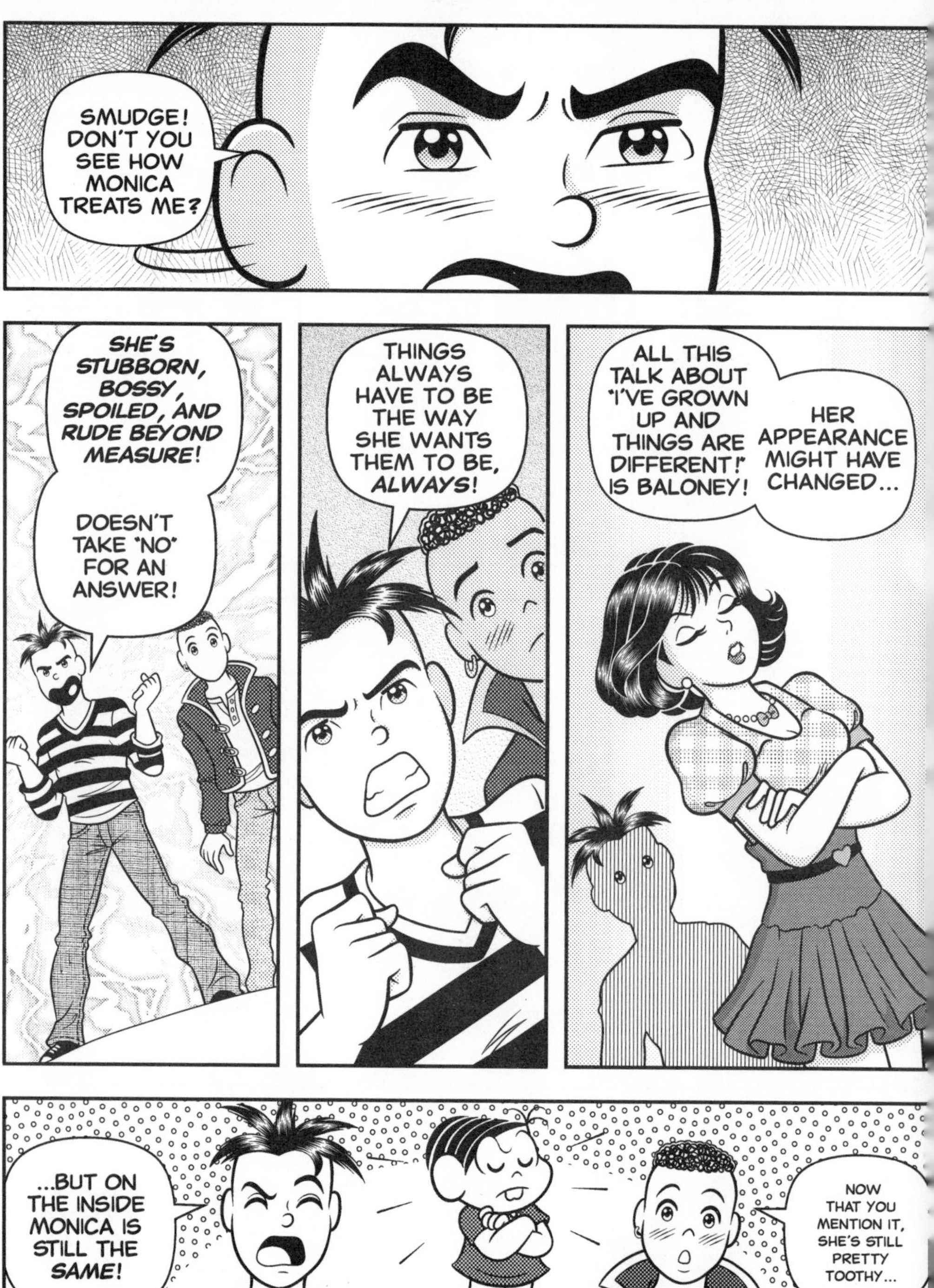
SMUDGE! DON'T YOU SEE HOW MONICA TREATS ME?
SHE'S STUBBORN, BOSSY, SPOILED, AND RUDE BEYOND MEASURE!
DOESN'T TAKE "NO" FOR AN ANSWER!
THINGS ALWAYS HAVE TO BE THE WAY SHE WANTS THEM TO BE, ALWAYS!
ALL THIS TALK ABOUT "I'VE GROWN UP AND THINGS ARE DIFFERENT!" IS BALONEY!
HER APPEARANCE MIGHT HAVE CHANGED...
...BUT ON THE INSIDE MONICA IS STILL THE SAME!
NOW THAT YOU MENTION IT, SHE'S STILL PRETTY TOOTHY...

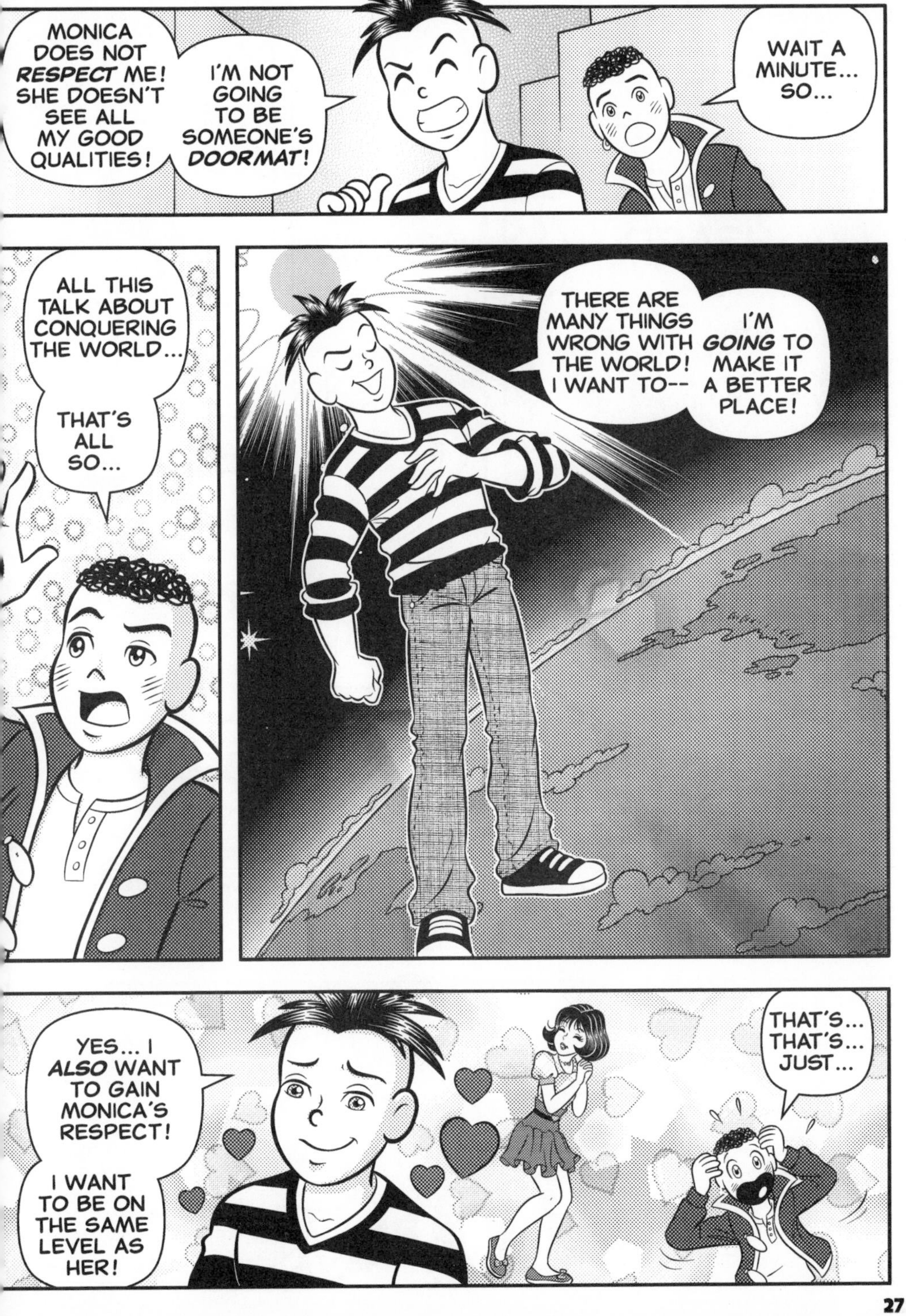
MONICA DOES NOT RESPECT ME! SHE DOESN'T SEE ALL MY GOOD QUALITIES!
I'M NOT GOING TO BE SOMEONE'S DOORMAT!
WAIT A MINUTE... SO...
ALL THIS TALK ABOUT CONQUERING THE WORLD...
THAT'S ALL SO...
THERE ARE MANY THINGS WRONG WITH THE WORLD! I WANT TO--
I'M GOING TO MAKE IT A BETTER PLACE!
YES... I ALSO WANT TO GAIN MONICA'S RESPECT!
I WANT TO BE ON THE SAME LEVEL AS HER!
THAT'S... THAT'S... JUST...

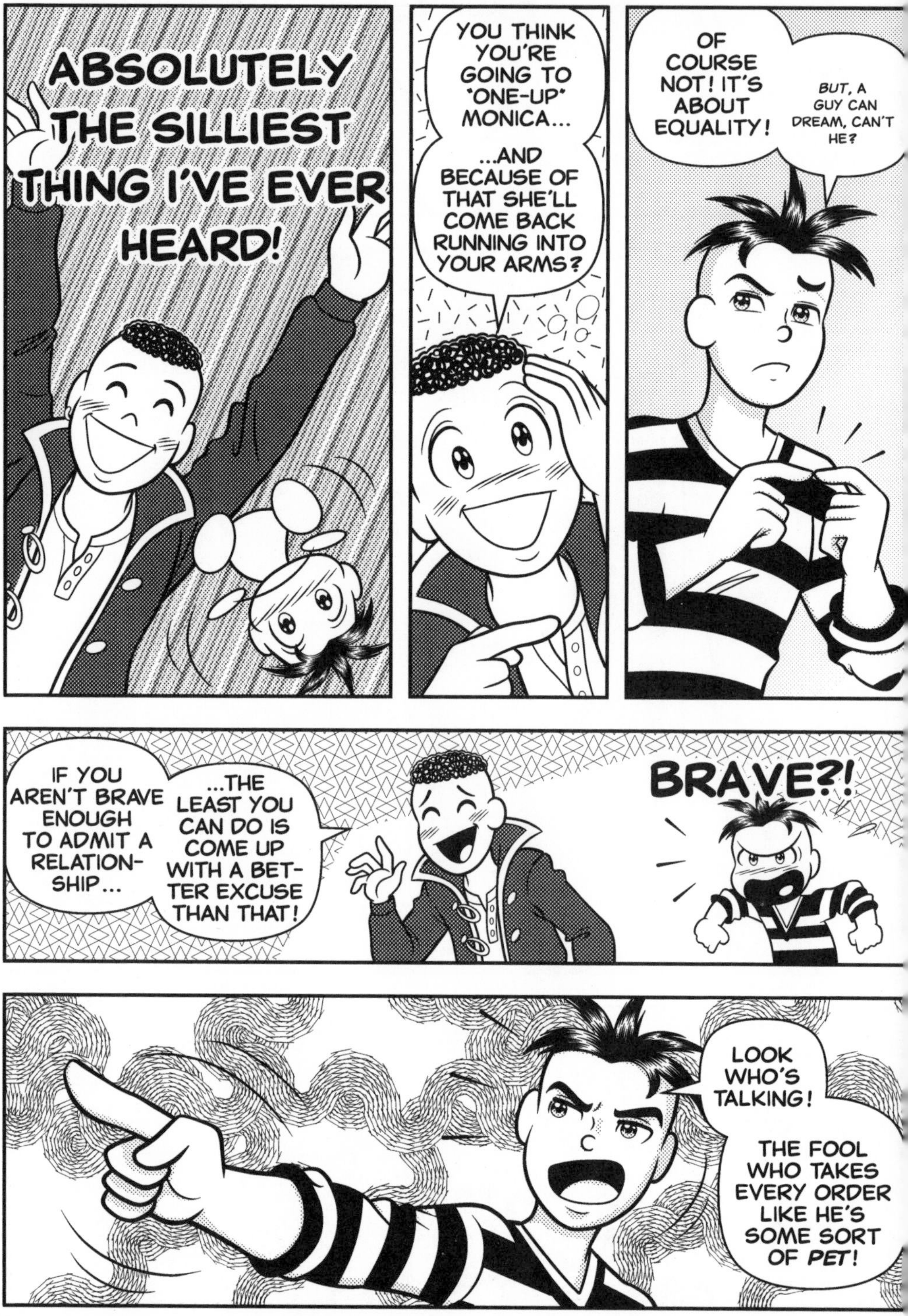
ABSOLUTELY THE SILLIEST THING I'VE EVER HEARD!
YOU THINK YOU'RE GOING TO "ONE-UP" MONICA...
...AND BECAUSE OF THAT SHE'LL COME BACK RUNNING INTO YOUR ARMS?
OF COURSE NOT! IT'S ABOUT EQUALITY!
BUT, A GUY CAN DREAM, CAN'T HE?
IF YOU AREN'T BRAVE ENOUGH TO ADMIT A RELATION-SHIP...
...THE LEAST YOU CAN DO IS COME UP WITH A BET-TER EXCUSE THAN THAT!
BRAVE?!
LOOK WHO'S TALKING!
THE FOOL WHO TAKES EVERY ORDER LIKE HE'S SOME SORT OF PET!

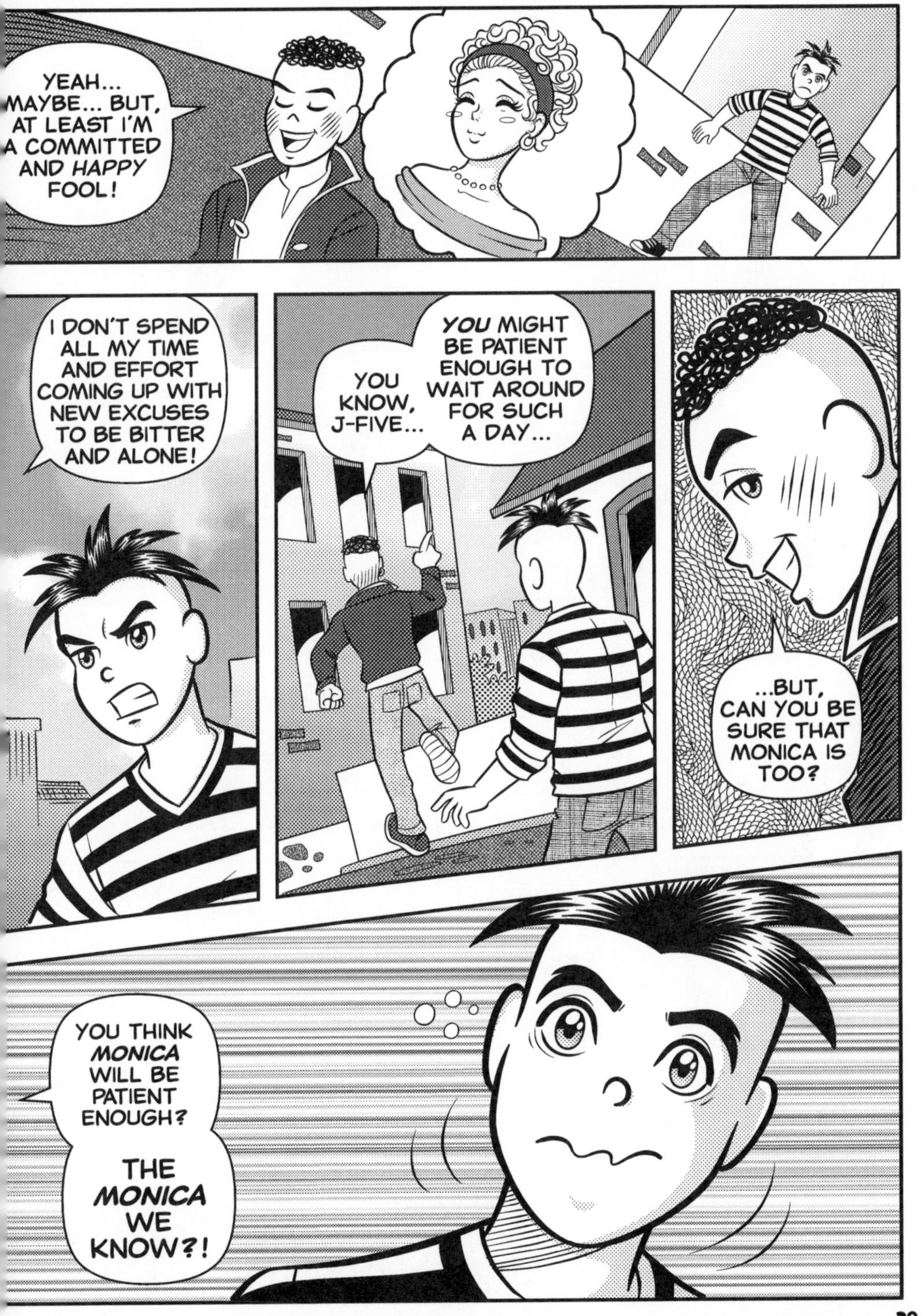
YEAH... MAYBE... BUT, AT LEAST I'M A COMMITTED AND *HAPPY* FOOL!
I DON'T SPEND ALL MY TIME AND EFFORT COMING UP WITH NEW EXCUSES TO BE BITTER AND ALONE!
YOU KNOW, J-FIVE...
YOU MIGHT BE PATIENT ENOUGH TO WAIT AROUND FOR SUCH A DAY...
...BUT, CAN YOU BE SURE THAT MONICA IS TOO?
YOU THINK *MONICA* WILL BE PATIENT ENOUGH?
THE *MONICA* WE KNOW?!

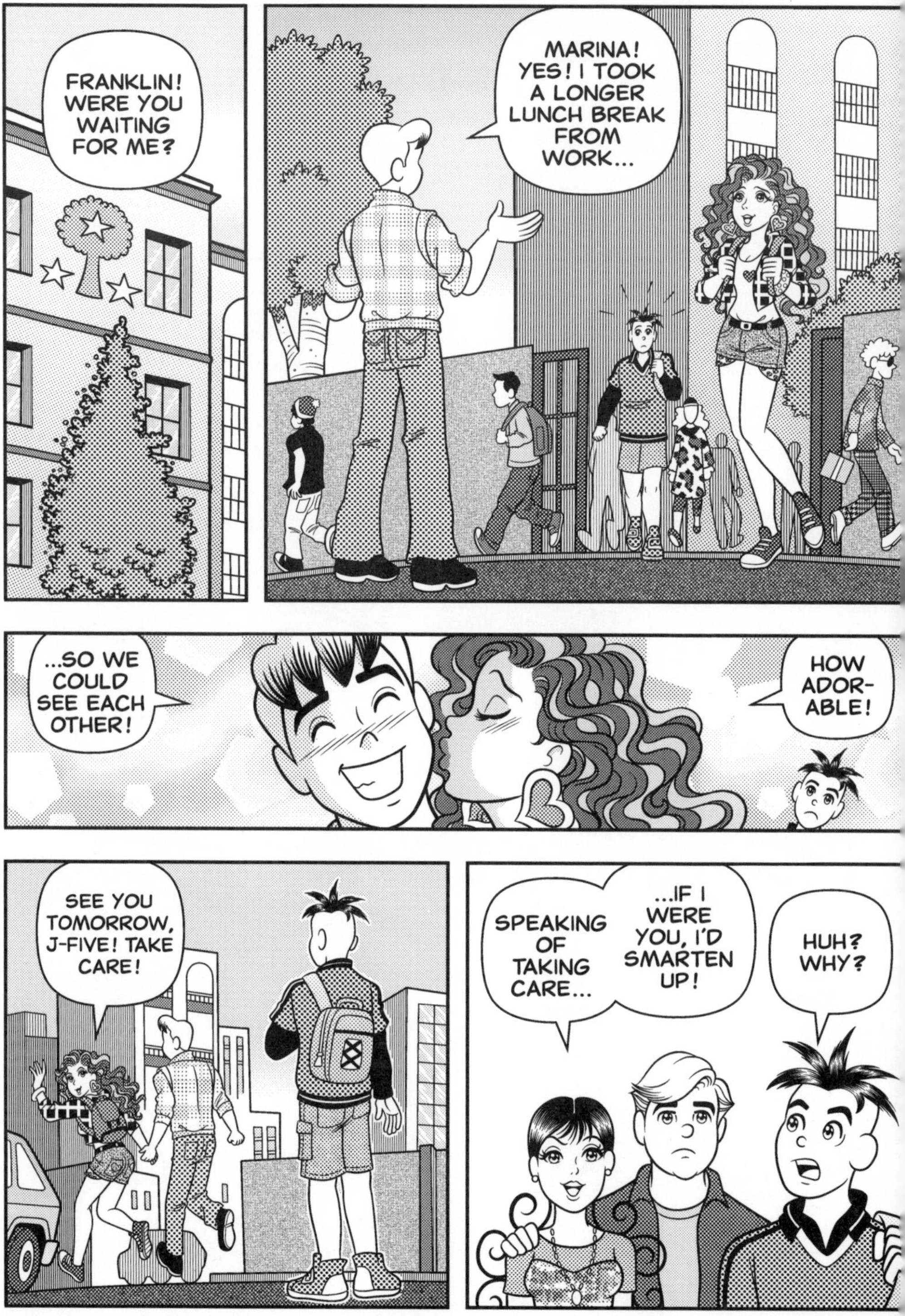
FRANKLIN! WERE YOU WAITING FOR ME?
MARINA! YES! I TOOK A LONGER LUNCH BREAK FROM WORK...
...SO WE COULD SEE EACH OTHER!
HOW ADOR-ABLE!
SEE YOU TOMORROW, J-FIVE! TAKE CARE!
SPEAKING OF TAKING CARE...
...IF I WERE YOU, I'D SMARTEN UP!
HUH? WHY?

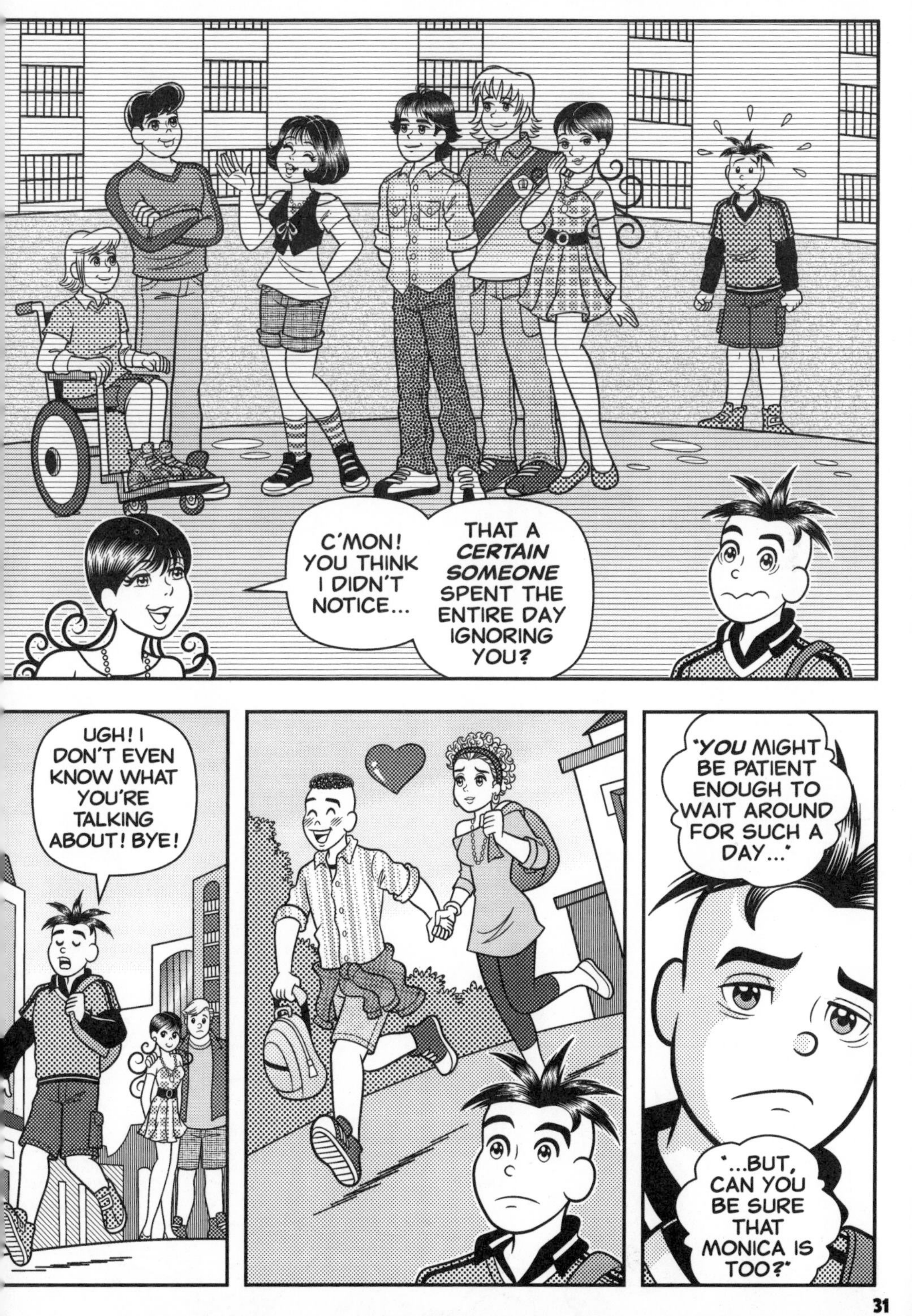

C'MON! YOU THINK I DIDN'T NOTICE...
THAT A *CERTAIN SOMEONE* SPENT THE ENTIRE DAY IGNORING YOU?
UGH! I DON'T EVEN KNOW WHAT YOU'RE TALKING ABOUT! BYE!
"*YOU* MIGHT BE PATIENT ENOUGH TO WAIT AROUND FOR SUCH A DAY..."
"...BUT, CAN YOU BE SURE THAT MONICA IS TOO?"

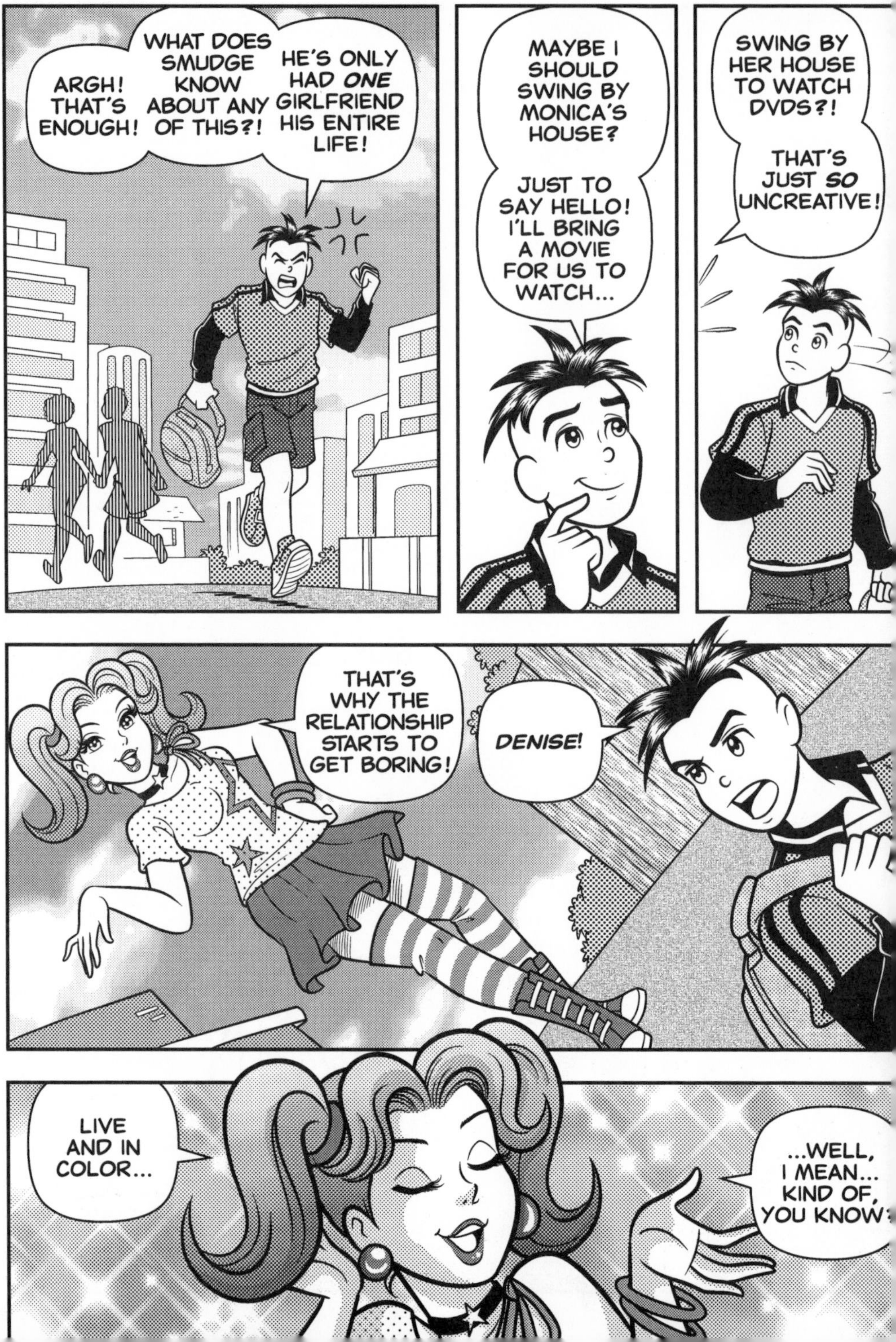
ARGH! THAT'S ENOUGH!
WHAT DOES SMUDGE KNOW ABOUT ANY OF THIS?!
HE'S ONLY HAD *ONE* GIRLFRIEND HIS ENTIRE LIFE!
MAYBE I SHOULD SWING BY MONICA'S HOUSE?
JUST TO SAY HELLO! I'LL BRING A MOVIE FOR US TO WATCH...
SWING BY HER HOUSE TO WATCH DVDS?!
THAT'S JUST *SO* UNCREATIVE!
THAT'S WHY THE RELATIONSHIP STARTS TO GET BORING!
DENISE!
LIVE AND IN COLOR...
...WELL, I MEAN... KIND OF, YOU KNOW

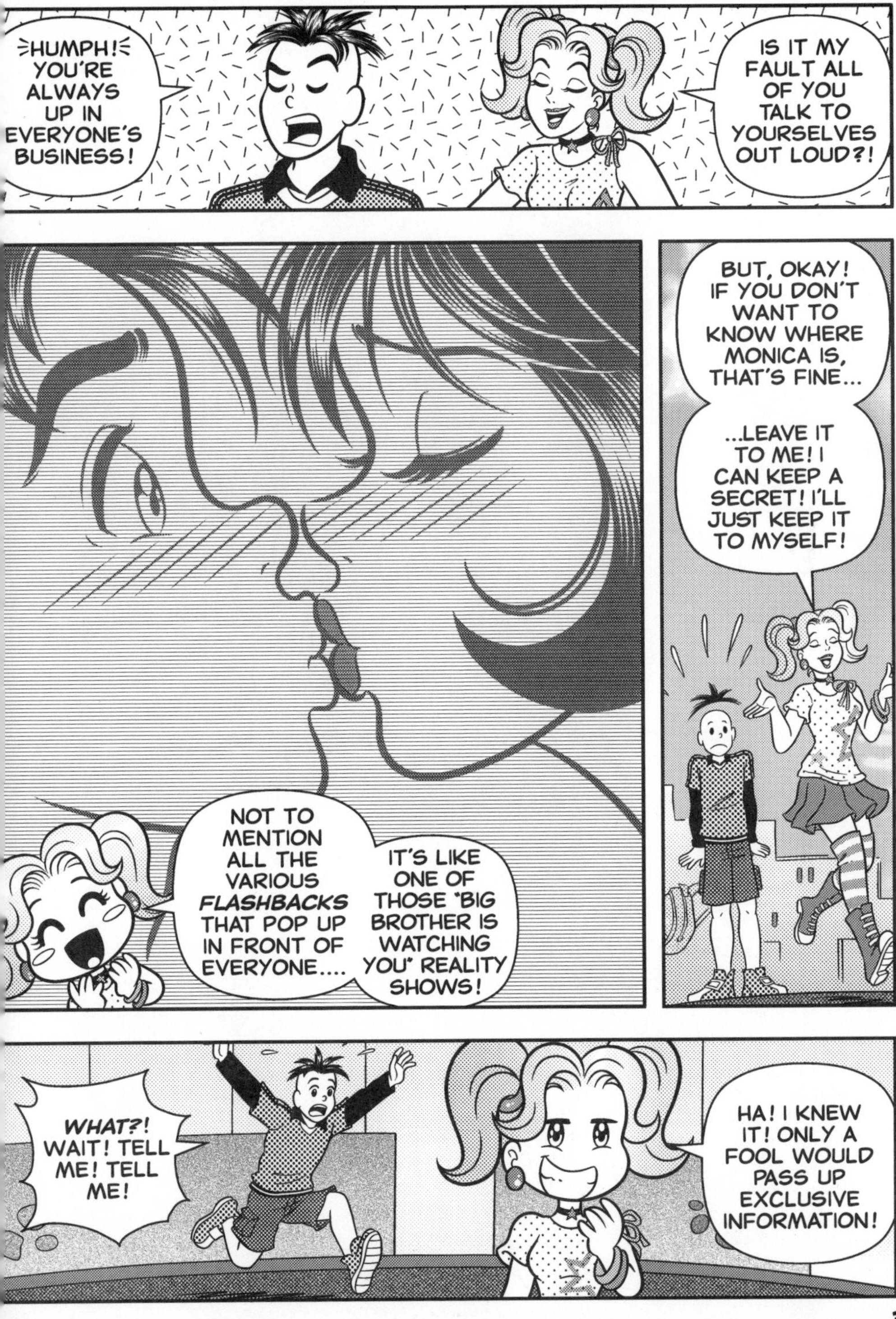
HUMPH! YOU'RE ALWAYS UP IN EVERYONE'S BUSINESS!
IS IT MY FAULT ALL OF YOU TALK TO YOURSELVES OUT LOUD?!
NOT TO MENTION ALL THE VARIOUS *FLASHBACKS* THAT POP UP IN FRONT OF EVERYONE....
IT'S LIKE ONE OF THOSE "BIG BROTHER IS WATCHING YOU" REALITY SHOWS!
BUT, OKAY! IF YOU DON'T WANT TO KNOW WHERE MONICA IS, THAT'S FINE...
...LEAVE IT TO ME! I CAN KEEP A SECRET! I'LL JUST KEEP IT TO MYSELF!
WHAT?! WAIT! TELL ME! TELL ME!
HA! I KNEW IT! ONLY A FOOL WOULD PASS UP EXCLUSIVE INFORMATION!

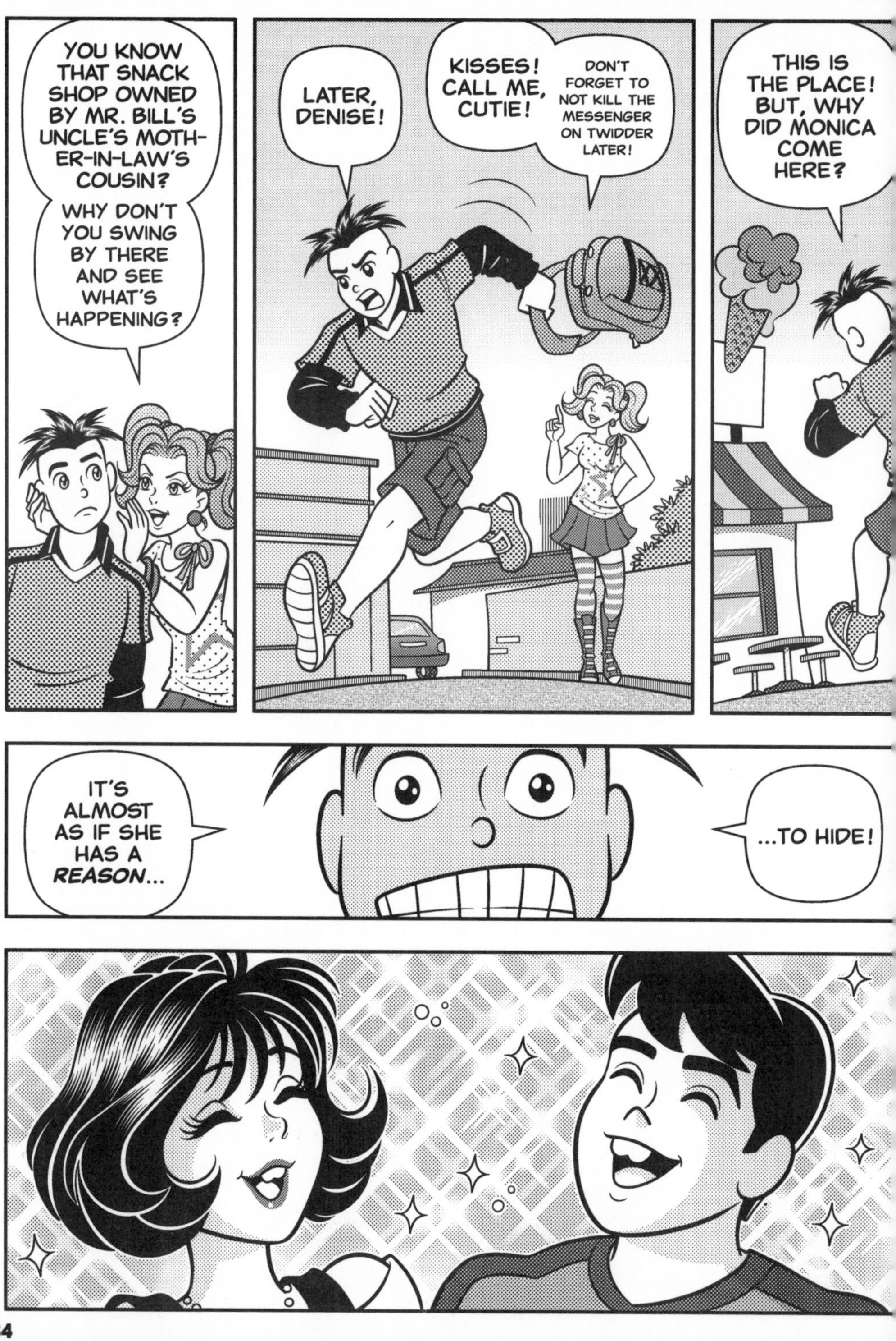

YOU KNOW THAT SNACK SHOP OWNED BY MR. BILL'S UNCLE'S MOTH-ER-IN-LAW'S COUSIN?
WHY DON'T YOU SWING BY THERE AND SEE WHAT'S HAPPENING?
LATER, DENISE!
KISSES! CALL ME, CUTIE!
DON'T FORGET TO NOT KILL THE MESSENGER ON TWIDDER LATER!
THIS IS THE PLACE! BUT, WHY DID MONICA COME HERE?
IT'S ALMOST AS IF SHE HAS A *REASON*...
...TO HIDE!

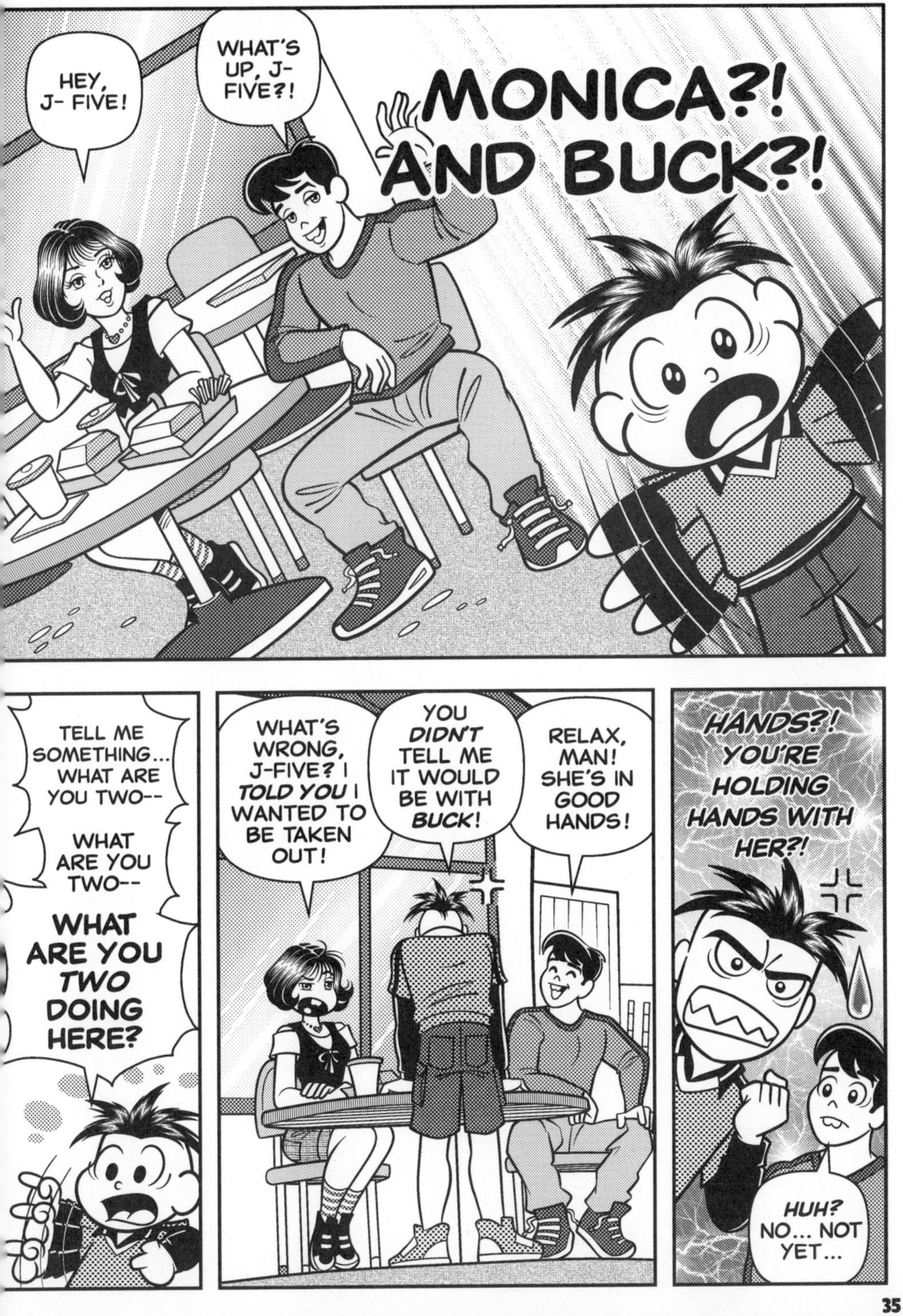
HEY, J- FIVE!
WHAT'S UP, J- FIVE?!
MONICA?! AND BUCK?!
TELL ME SOMETHING... WHAT ARE YOU TWO--
WHAT ARE YOU TWO--
WHAT ARE YOU TWO DOING HERE?
WHAT'S WRONG, J-FIVE? I TOLD YOU I WANTED TO BE TAKEN OUT!
YOU DIDN'T TELL ME IT WOULD BE WITH BUCK!
RELAX, MAN! SHE'S IN GOOD HANDS!
HANDS?! YOU'RE HOLDING HANDS WITH HER?!
HUH? NO... NOT YET...

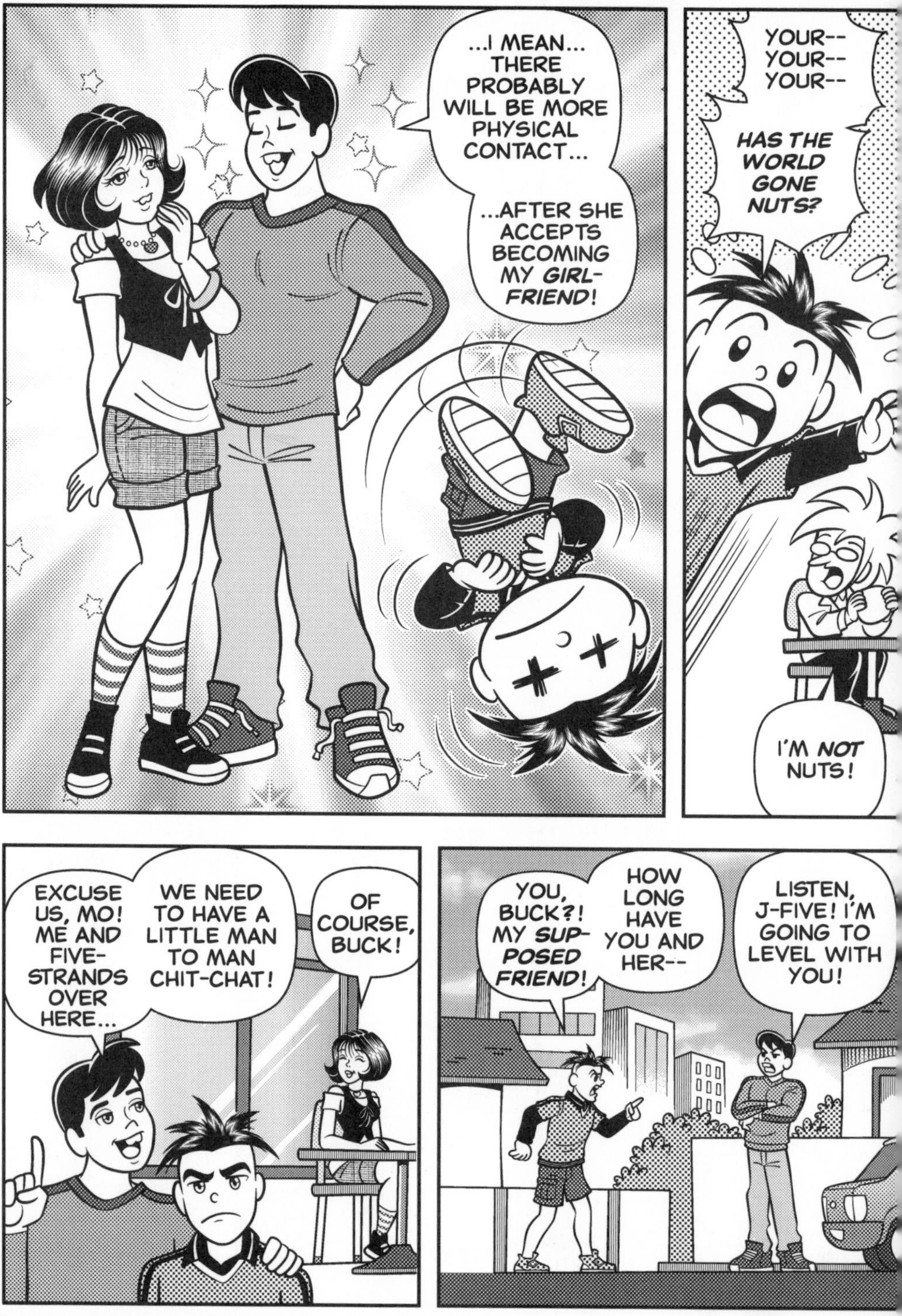
...I MEAN... THERE PROBABLY WILL BE MORE PHYSICAL CONTACT...
...AFTER SHE ACCEPTS BECOMING MY GIRL-FRIEND!
YOUR-- YOUR-- YOUR--
HAS THE WORLD GONE NUTS?
I'M NOT NUTS!
EXCUSE US, MO! ME AND FIVE-STRANDS OVER HERE...
WE NEED TO HAVE A LITTLE MAN TO MAN CHIT-CHAT!
OF COURSE, BUCK!
YOU, BUCK?! MY SUP-POSED FRIEND!
HOW LONG HAVE YOU AND HER--
LISTEN, J-FIVE! I'M GOING TO LEVEL WITH YOU!

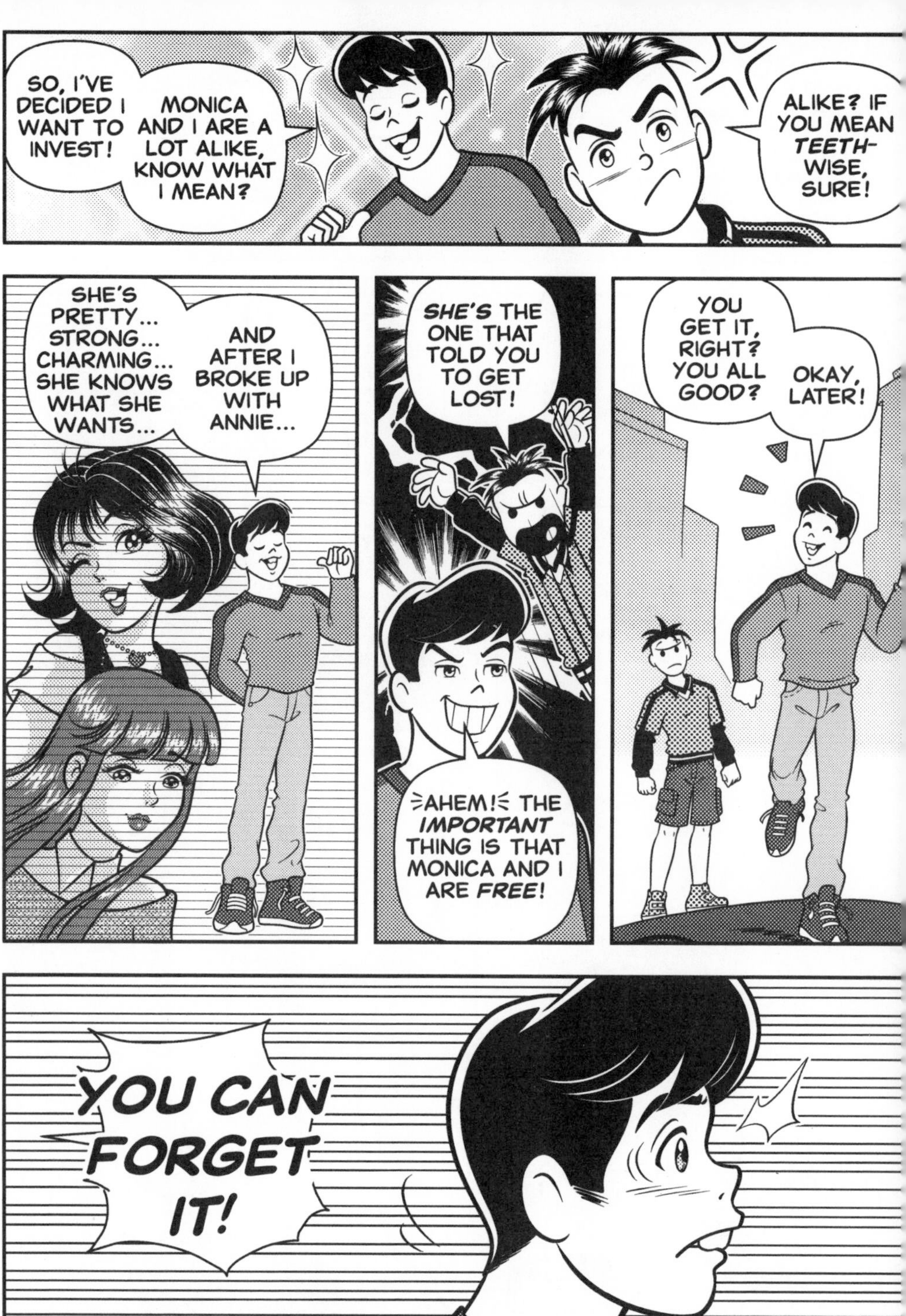

SO, I'VE DECIDED I WANT TO INVEST!
MONICA AND I ARE A LOT ALIKE, KNOW WHAT I MEAN?
ALIKE? IF YOU MEAN *TEETH*-WISE, SURE!
SHE'S PRETTY... STRONG... CHARMING... SHE KNOWS WHAT SHE WANTS...
AND AFTER I BROKE UP WITH ANNIE...
SHE'S THE ONE THAT TOLD YOU TO GET LOST!
AHEM! THE *IMPORTANT* THING IS THAT MONICA AND I ARE *FREE*!
YOU GET IT, RIGHT? YOU ALL GOOD?
OKAY, LATER!
YOU CAN FORGET IT!

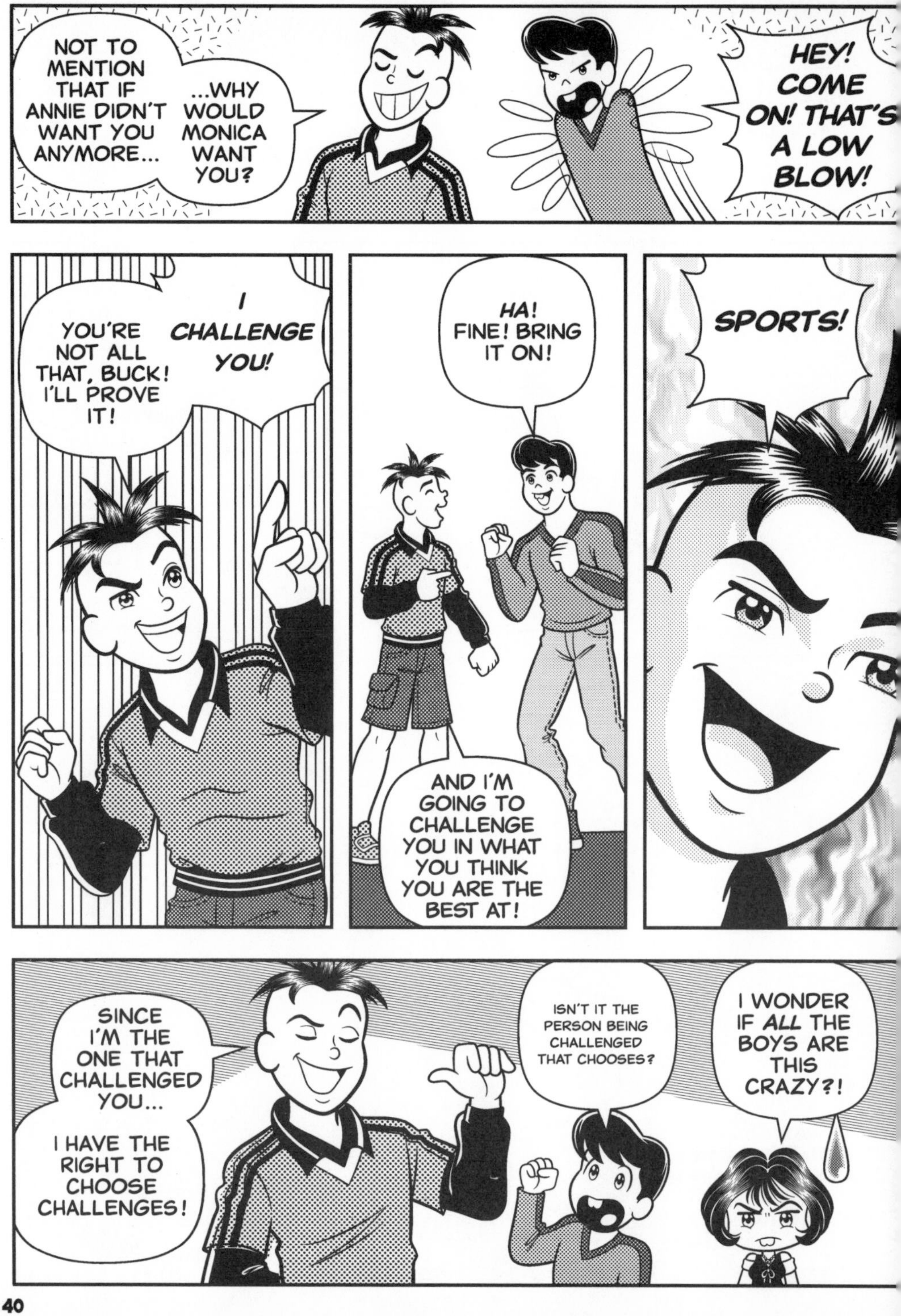
NOT TO MENTION THAT IF ANNIE DIDN'T WANT YOU ANYMORE...
...WHY WOULD MONICA WANT YOU?
HEY! COME ON! THAT'S A LOW BLOW!
YOU'RE NOT ALL THAT, BUCK! I'LL PROVE IT!
I CHALLENGE YOU!
HA! FINE! BRING IT ON!
AND I'M GOING TO CHALLENGE YOU IN WHAT YOU THINK YOU ARE THE BEST AT!
SPORTS!
SINCE I'M THE ONE THAT CHALLENGED YOU...
I HAVE THE RIGHT TO CHOOSE CHALLENGES!
ISN'T IT THE PERSON BEING CHALLENGED THAT CHOOSES?
I WONDER IF ALL THE BOYS ARE THIS CRAZY?!

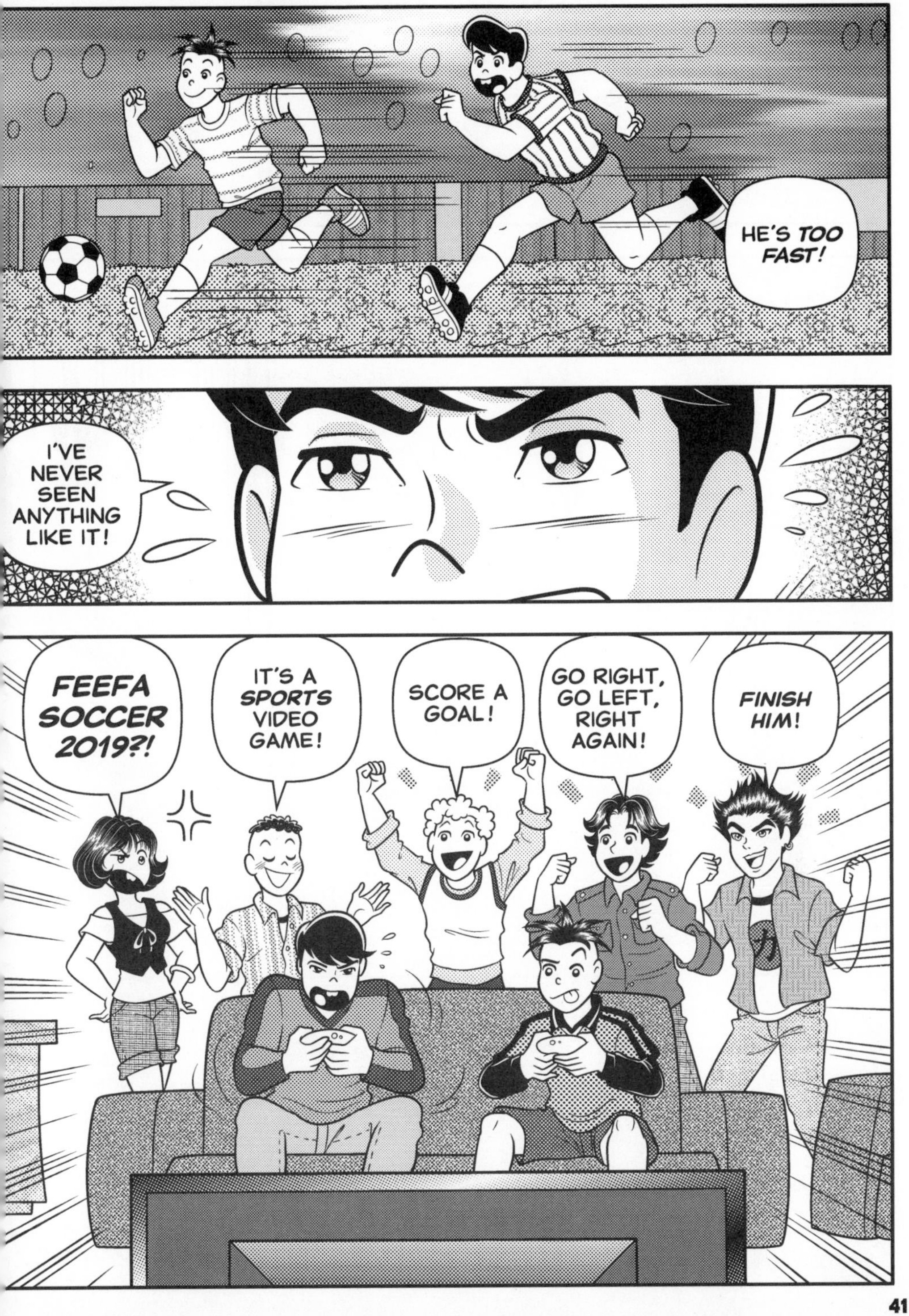
HE'S *TOO FAST*!
I'VE NEVER SEEN ANYTHING LIKE IT!
FEEFA SOCCER 2019?!
IT'S A *SPORTS* VIDEO GAME!
SCORE A GOAL!
GO RIGHT, GO LEFT, RIGHT AGAIN!
FINISH HIM!

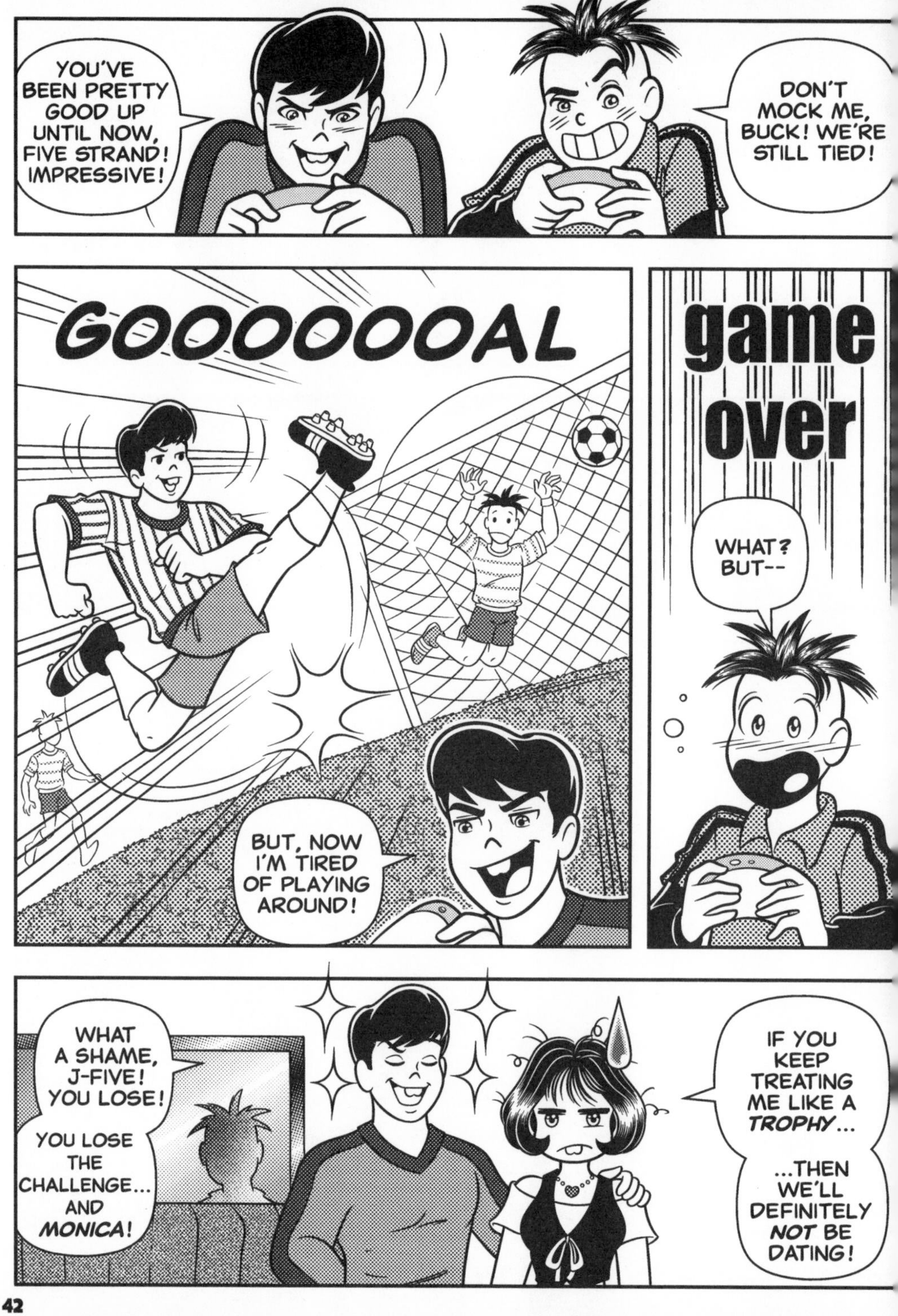
YOU'VE BEEN PRETTY GOOD UP UNTIL NOW, FIVE STRAND! IMPRESSIVE!
DON'T MOCK ME, BUCK! WE'RE STILL TIED!
GOOOOOOAL
BUT, NOW I'M TIRED OF PLAYING AROUND!
game over
WHAT? BUT--
WHAT A SHAME, J-FIVE! YOU LOSE!
YOU LOSE THE CHALLENGE... AND *MONICA*!
IF YOU KEEP TREATING ME LIKE A *TROPHY*...
...THEN WE'LL DEFINITELY *NOT* BE DATING!

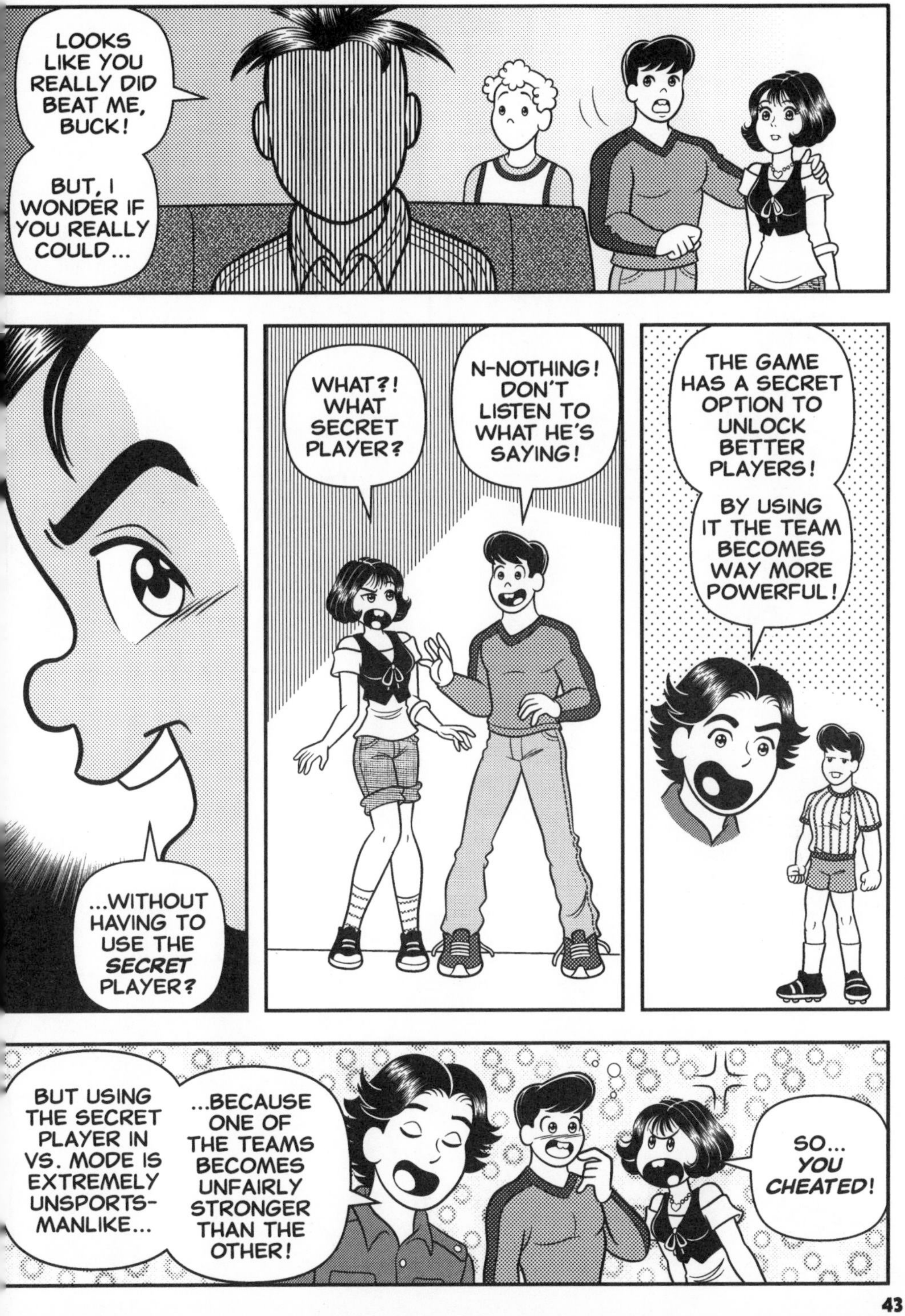
LOOKS LIKE YOU REALLY DID BEAT ME, BUCK!
BUT, I WONDER IF YOU REALLY COULD...
...WITHOUT HAVING TO USE THE *SECRET* PLAYER?
WHAT?! WHAT SECRET PLAYER?
N-NOTHING! DON'T LISTEN TO WHAT HE'S SAYING!
THE GAME HAS A SECRET OPTION TO UNLOCK BETTER PLAYERS!
BY USING IT THE TEAM BECOMES WAY MORE POWERFUL!
BUT USING THE SECRET PLAYER IN VS. MODE IS EXTREMELY UNSPORTS-MANLIKE...
...BECAUSE ONE OF THE TEAMS BECOMES UNFAIRLY STRONGER THAN THE OTHER!
SO... *YOU CHEATED*!

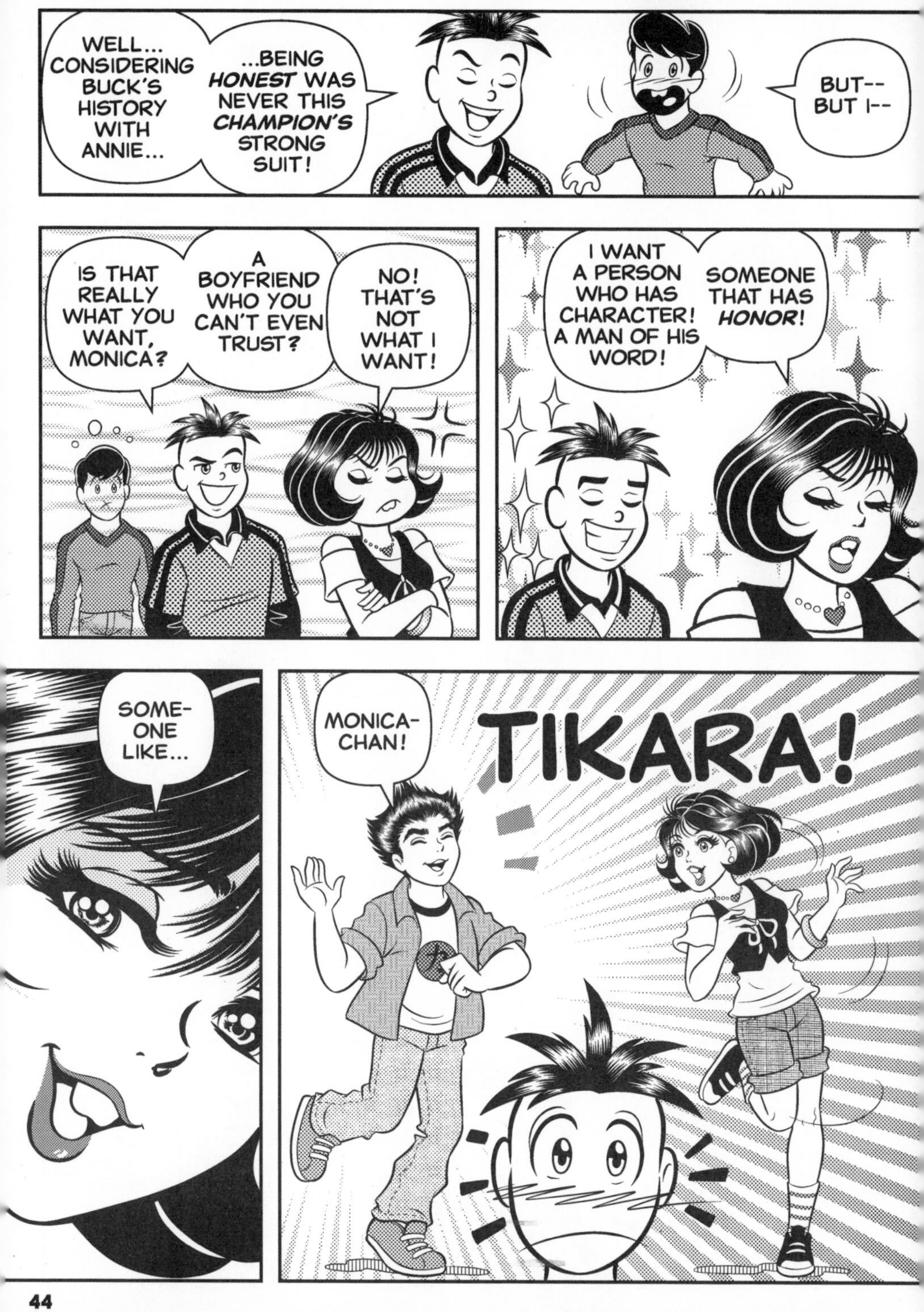
WELL... CONSIDERING BUCK'S HISTORY WITH ANNIE...
...BEING HONEST WAS NEVER THIS CHAMPION'S STRONG SUIT!
BUT-- BUT I--
IS THAT REALLY WHAT YOU WANT, MONICA?
A BOYFRIEND WHO YOU CAN'T EVEN TRUST?
NO! THAT'S NOT WHAT I WANT!
I WANT A PERSON WHO HAS CHARACTER! A MAN OF HIS WORD!
SOMEONE THAT HAS HONOR!
SOME-ONE LIKE...
MONICA-CHAN!
TIKARA!

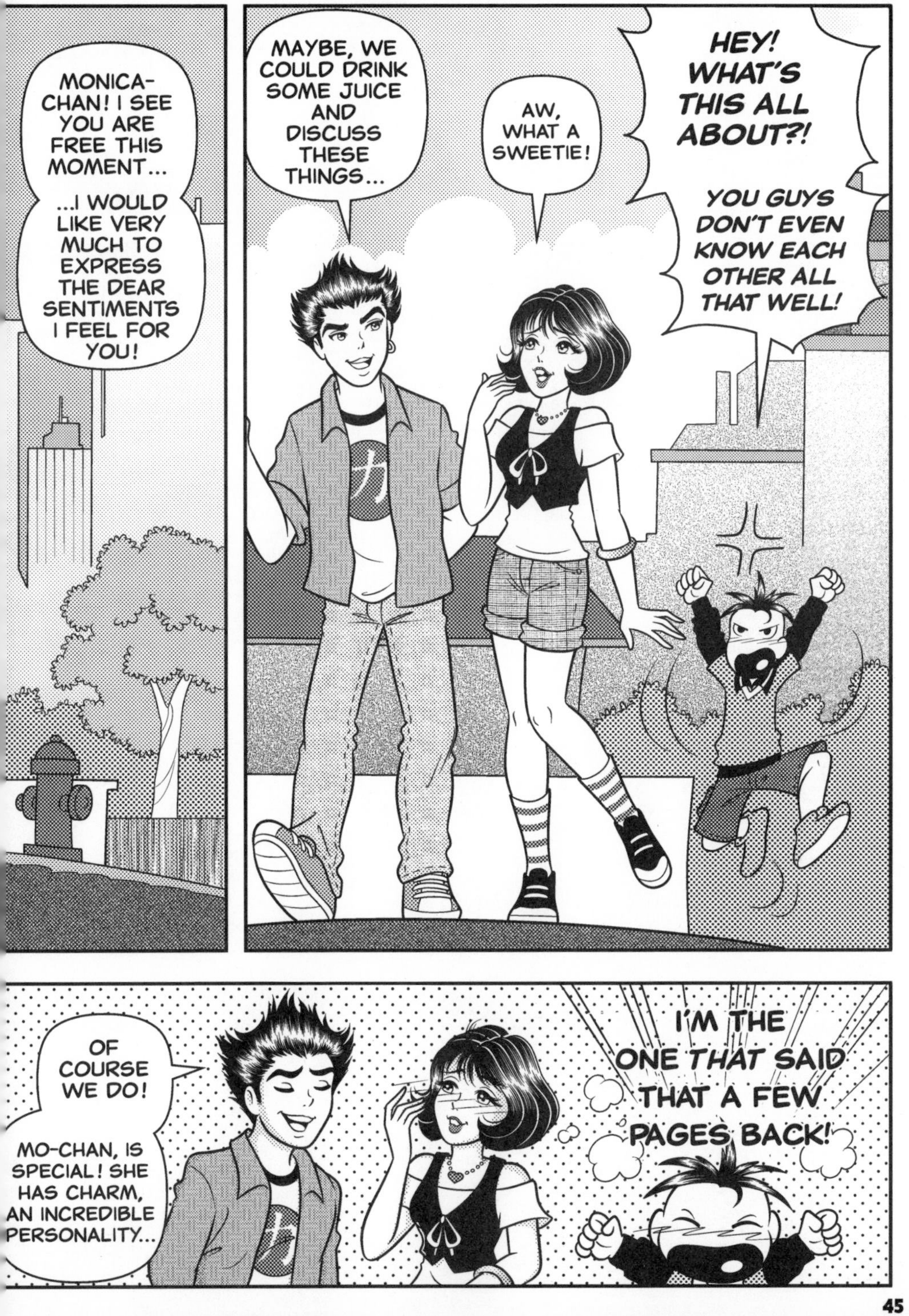
MONICA-CHAN! I SEE YOU ARE FREE THIS MOMENT...
...I WOULD LIKE VERY MUCH TO EXPRESS THE DEAR SENTIMENTS I FEEL FOR YOU!
MAYBE, WE COULD DRINK SOME JUICE AND DISCUSS THESE THINGS...
AW, WHAT A SWEETIE!
HEY! WHAT'S THIS ALL ABOUT?!
YOU GUYS DON'T EVEN KNOW EACH OTHER ALL THAT WELL!
OF COURSE WE DO!
MO-CHAN, IS SPECIAL! SHE HAS CHARM, AN INCREDIBLE PERSONALITY...
I'M THE ONE THAT SAID THAT A FEW PAGES BACK!

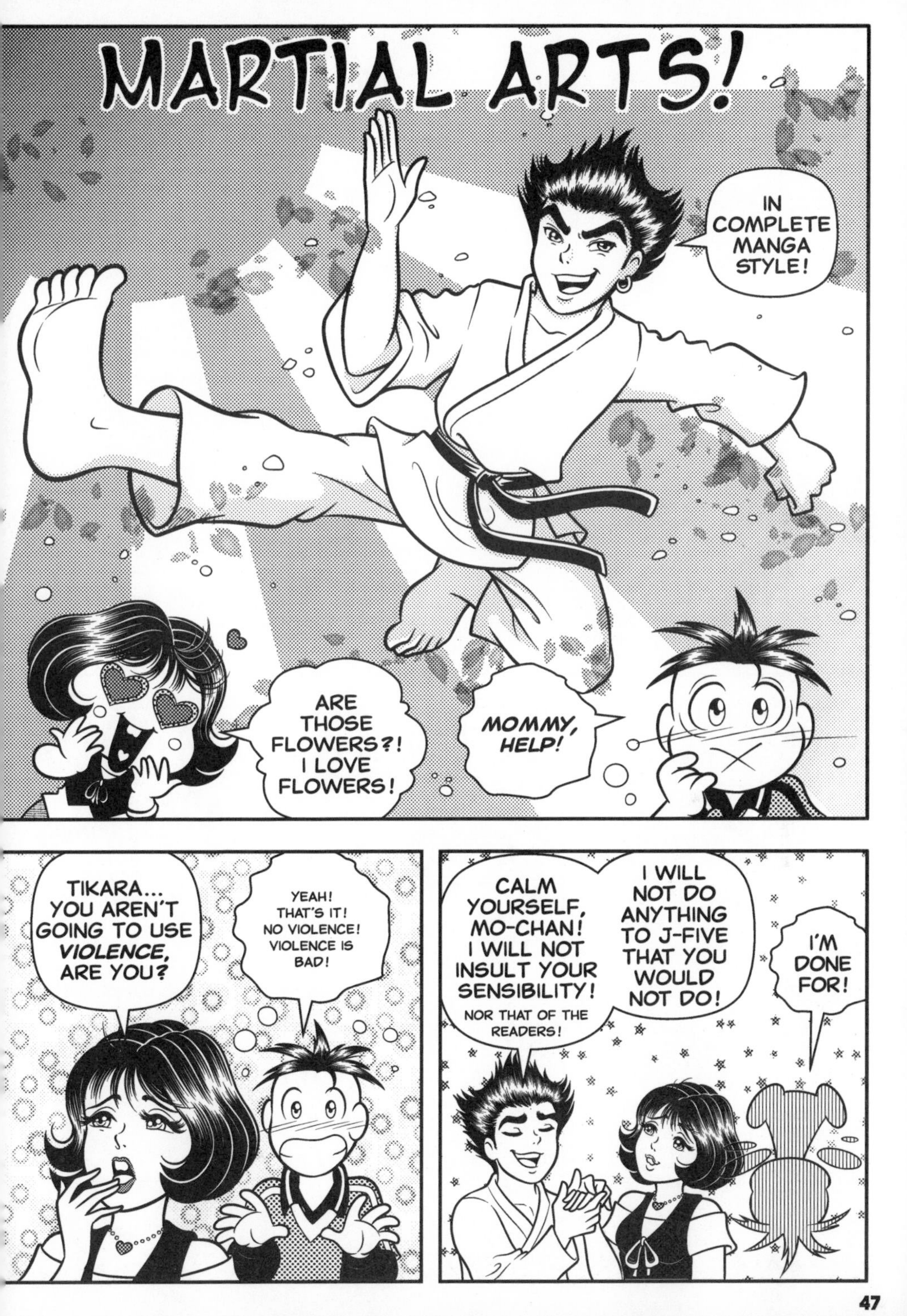
MARTIAL ARTS!
IN COMPLETE MANGA STYLE!
ARE THOSE FLOWERS?! I LOVE FLOWERS!
MOMMY, HELP!
TIKARA... YOU AREN'T GOING TO USE VIOLENCE, ARE YOU?
YEAH! THAT'S IT! NO VIOLENCE! VIOLENCE IS BAD!
CALM YOURSELF, MO-CHAN! I WILL NOT INSULT YOUR SENSIBILITY!
NOR THAT OF THE READERS!
I WILL NOT DO ANYTHING TO J-FIVE THAT YOU WOULD NOT DO!
I'M DONE FOR!

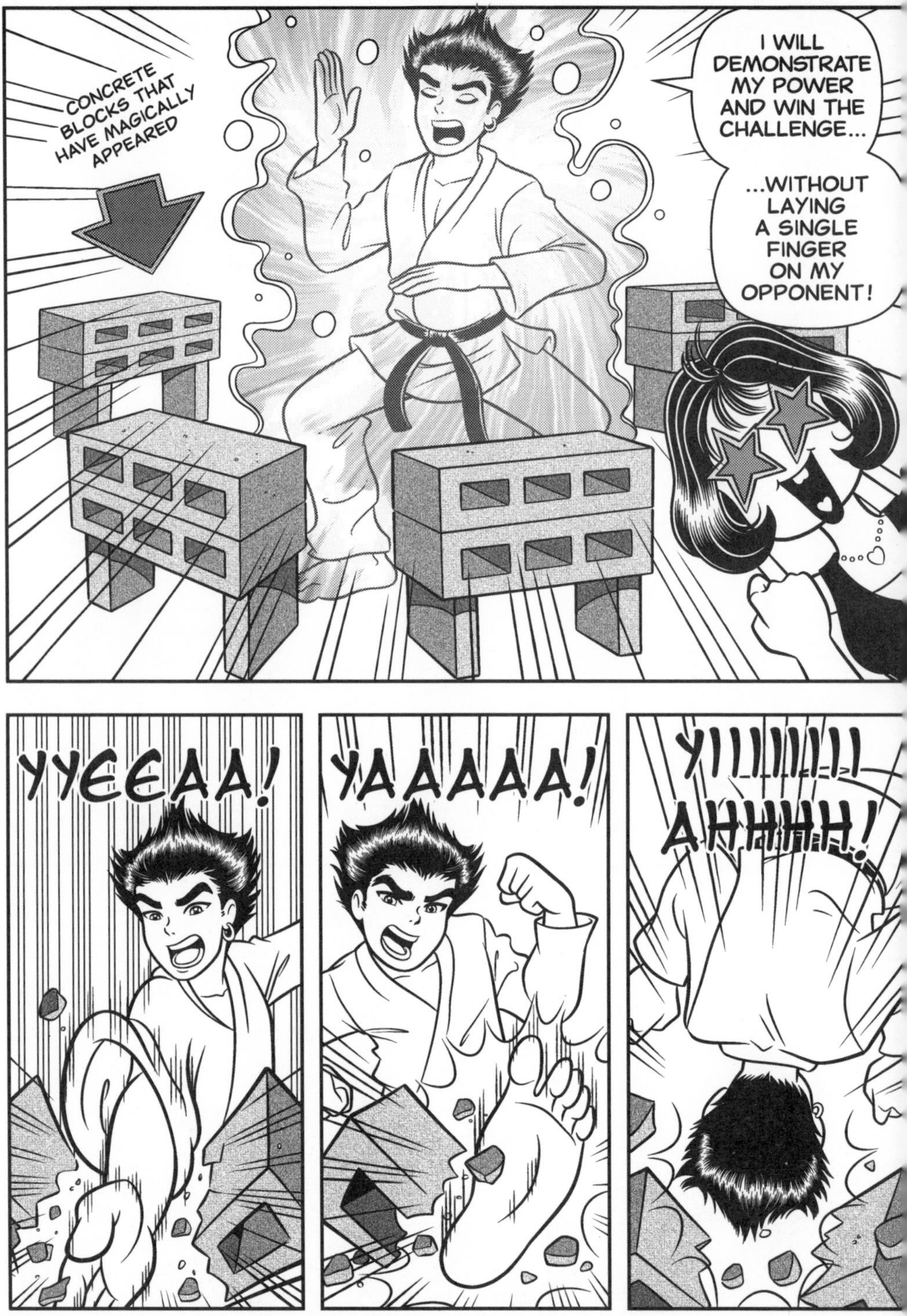
CONCRETE BLOCKS THAT HAVE MAGICALLY APPEARED
I WILL DEMONSTRATE MY POWER AND WIN THE CHALLENGE...
...WITHOUT LAYING A SINGLE FINGER ON MY OPPONENT!
YYEEAA!
YAAAAA!
YIIIIIIII AHHHH!

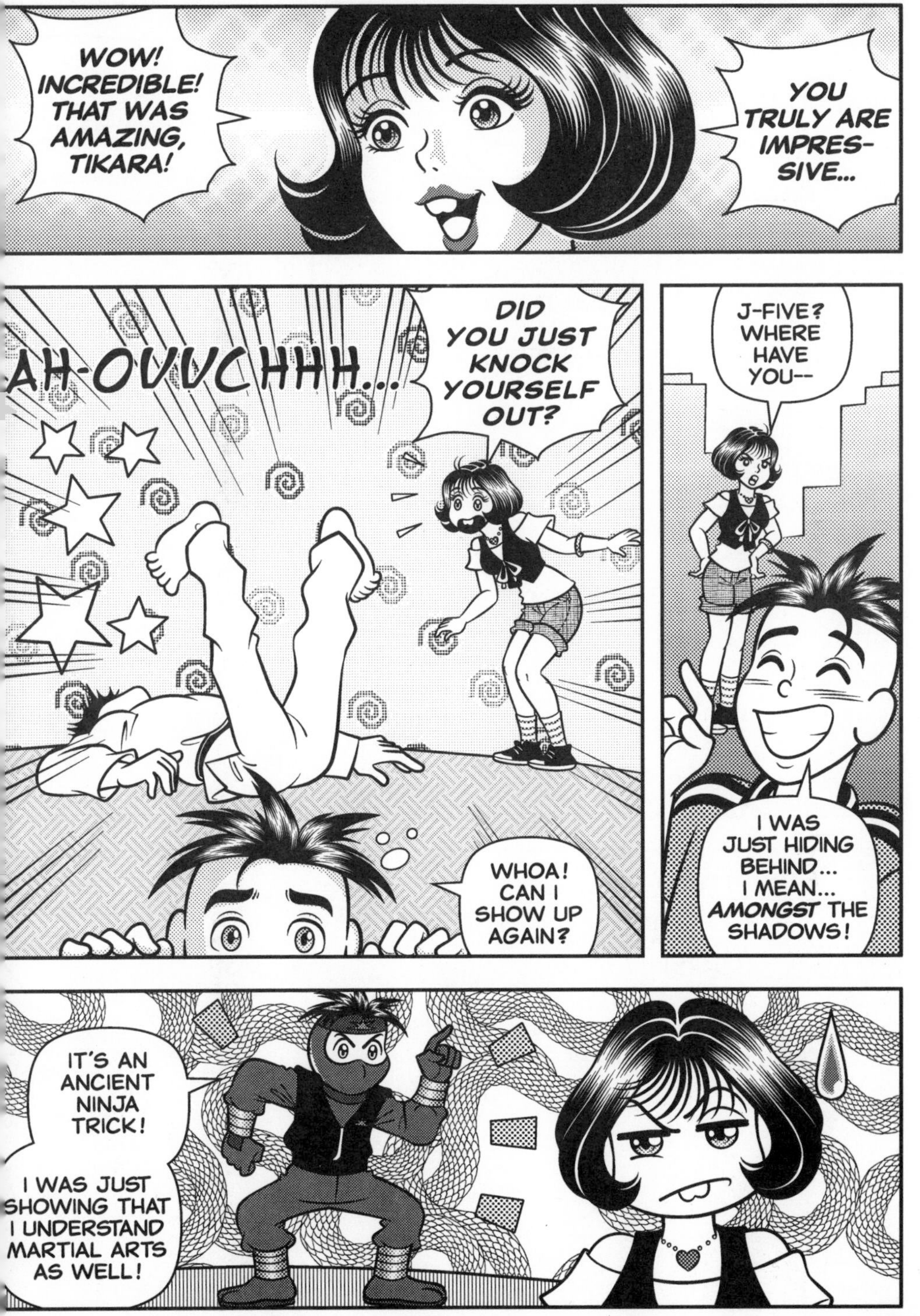
WOW! INCREDIBLE! THAT WAS AMAZING, TIKARA!
YOU TRULY ARE IMPRES-SIVE...
AH-OUUCHHH...
DID YOU JUST KNOCK YOURSELF OUT?
WHOA! CAN I SHOW UP AGAIN?
J-FIVE? WHERE HAVE YOU--
I WAS JUST HIDING BEHIND... I MEAN... AMONGST THE SHADOWS!
IT'S AN ANCIENT NINJA TRICK!
I WAS JUST SHOWING THAT I UNDERSTAND MARTIAL ARTS AS WELL!

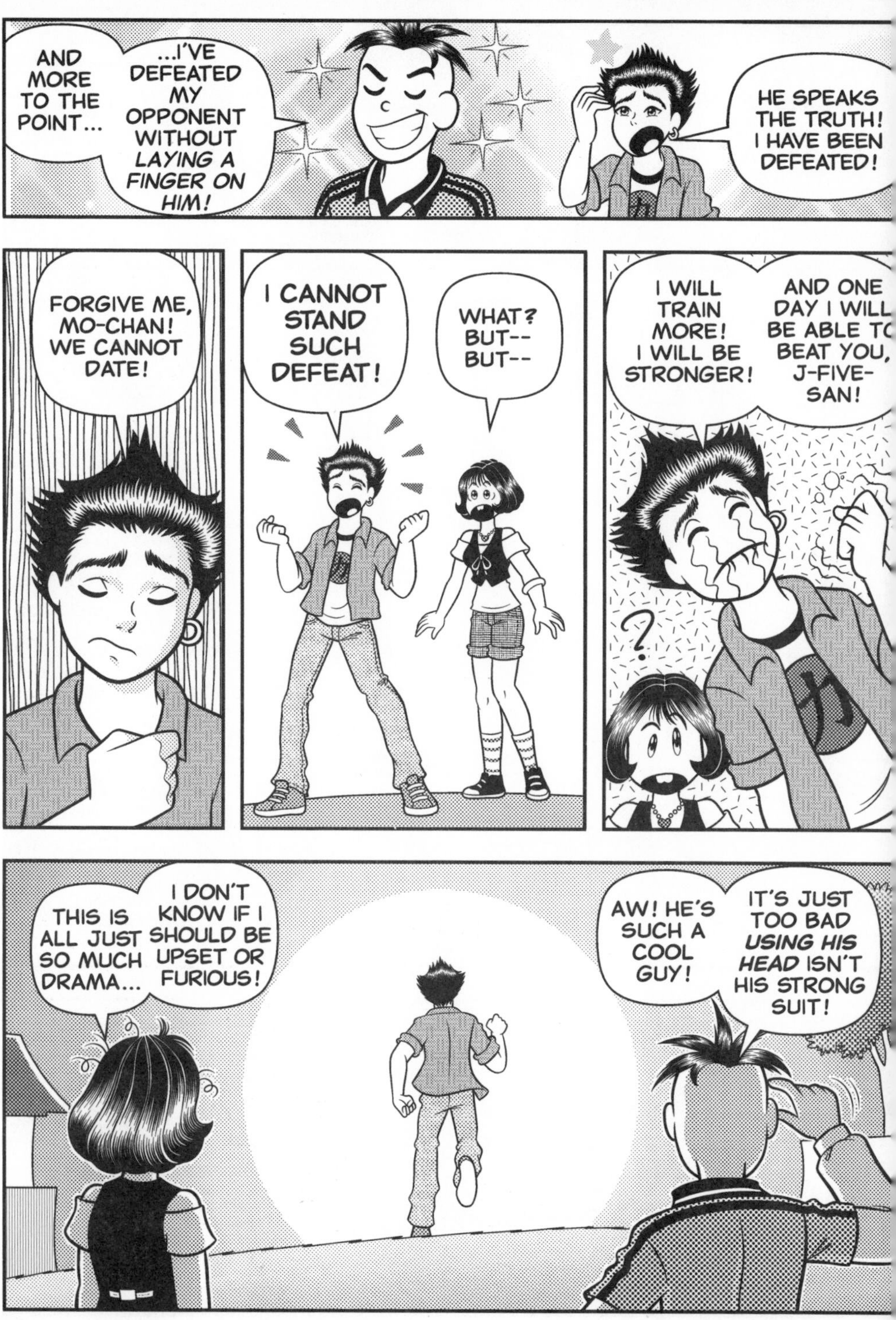
AND MORE TO THE POINT...
...I'VE DEFEATED MY OPPONENT WITHOUT *LAYING A FINGER ON HIM!*
HE SPEAKS THE TRUTH! I HAVE BEEN DEFEATED!
FORGIVE ME, MO-CHAN! WE CANNOT DATE!
I CANNOT STAND SUCH DEFEAT!
WHAT? BUT-- BUT--
I WILL TRAIN MORE! I WILL BE STRONGER!
AND ONE DAY I WILL BE ABLE TO BEAT YOU, J-FIVE-SAN!
THIS IS ALL JUST SO MUCH DRAMA...
I DON'T KNOW IF I SHOULD BE UPSET OR FURIOUS!
AW! HE'S SUCH A COOL GUY!
IT'S JUST TOO BAD *USING HIS HEAD* ISN'T HIS STRONG SUIT!

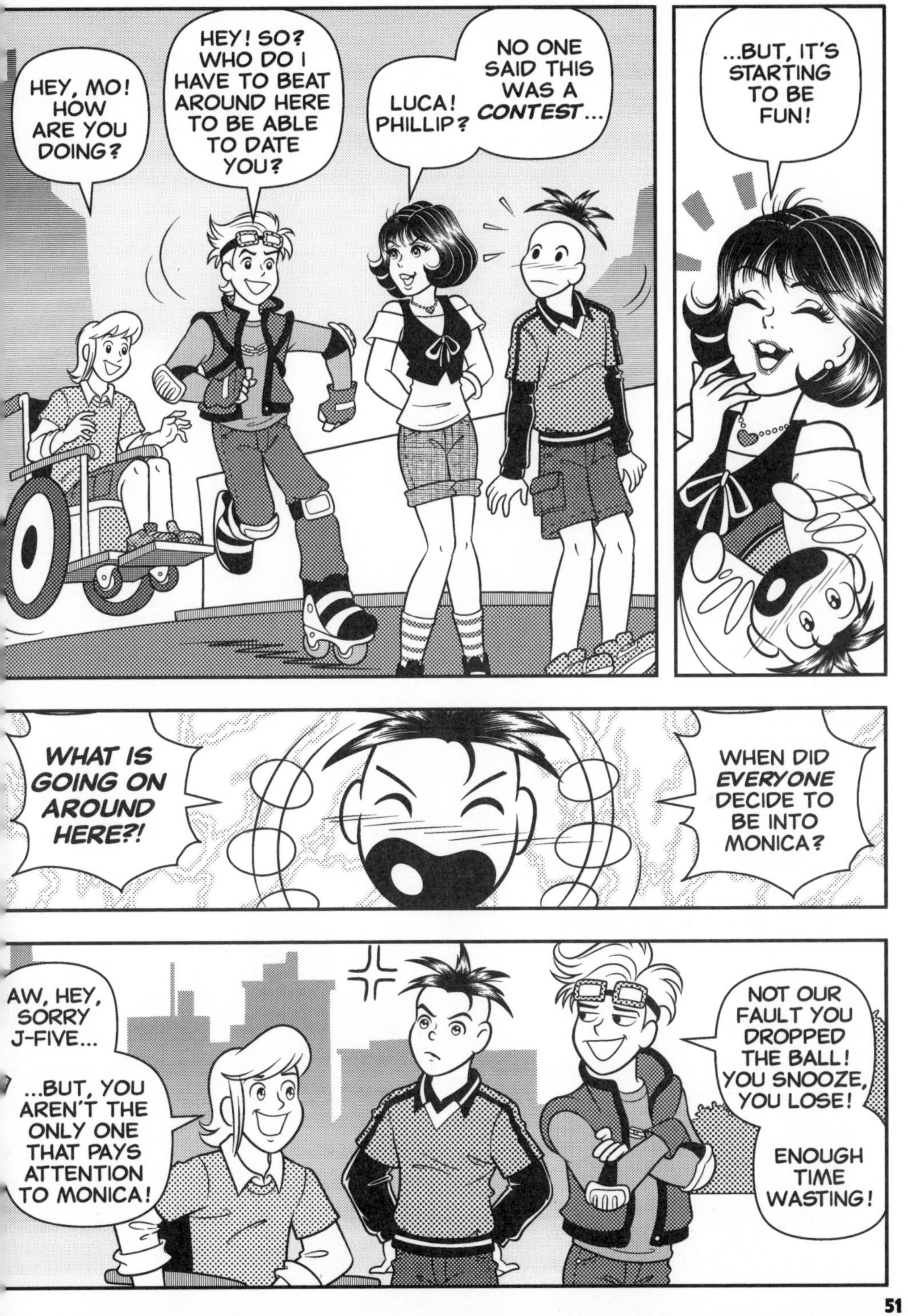
HEY, MO! HOW ARE YOU DOING?
HEY! SO? WHO DO I HAVE TO BEAT AROUND HERE TO BE ABLE TO DATE YOU?
LUCA! PHILLIP?
NO ONE SAID THIS WAS A CONTEST...
...BUT, IT'S STARTING TO BE FUN!
WHAT IS GOING ON AROUND HERE?!
WHEN DID EVERYONE DECIDE TO BE INTO MONICA?
AW, HEY, SORRY J-FIVE...
...BUT, YOU AREN'T THE ONLY ONE THAT PAYS ATTENTION TO MONICA!
NOT OUR FAULT YOU DROPPED THE BALL! YOU SNOOZE, YOU LOSE!
ENOUGH TIME WASTING!

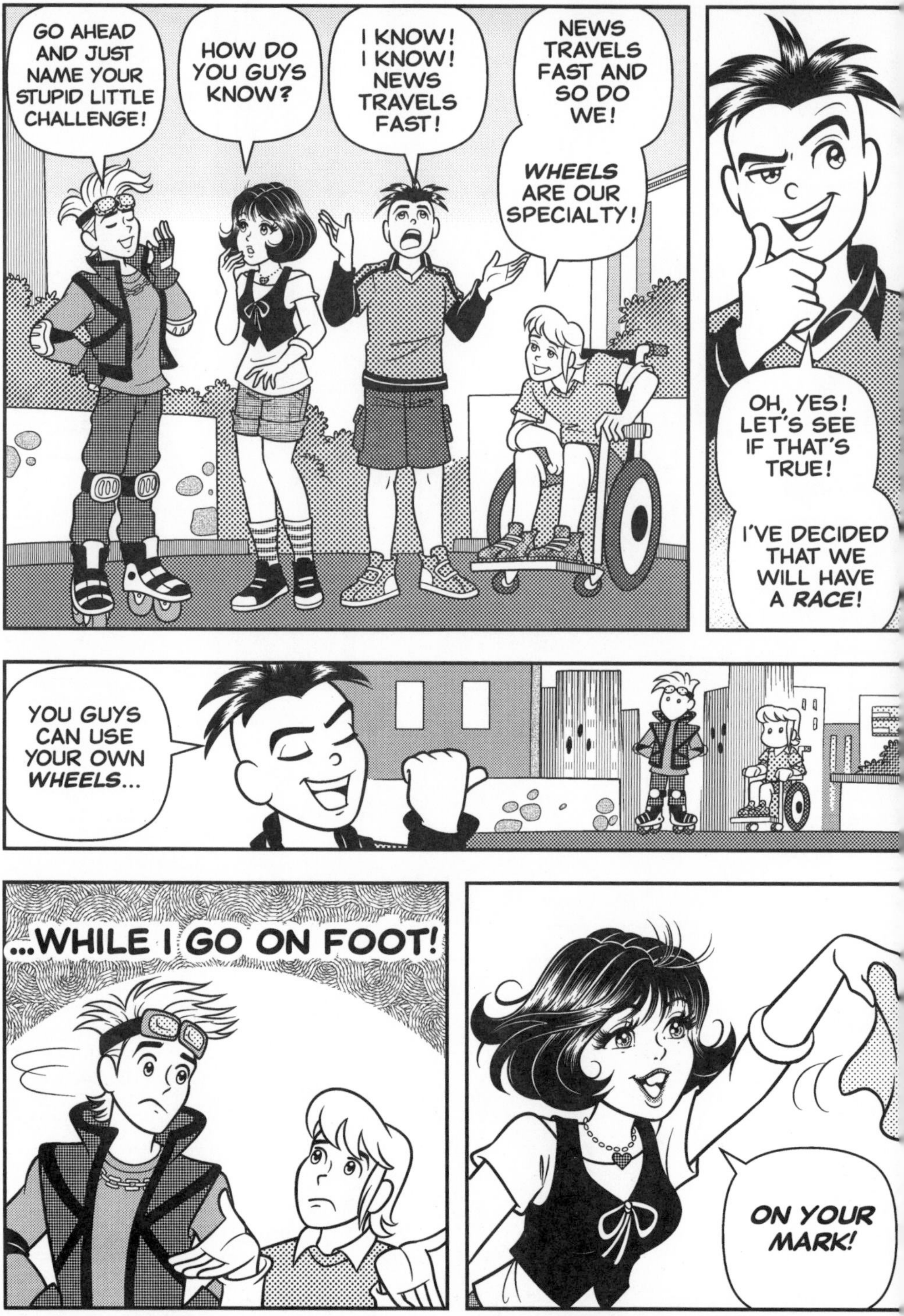
GO AHEAD AND JUST NAME YOUR STUPID LITTLE CHALLENGE!
HOW DO YOU GUYS KNOW?
I KNOW! I KNOW! NEWS TRAVELS FAST!
NEWS TRAVELS FAST AND SO DO WE!
WHEELS ARE OUR SPECIALTY!
OH, YES! LET'S SEE IF THAT'S TRUE!
I'VE DECIDED THAT WE WILL HAVE A *RACE*!
YOU GUYS CAN USE YOUR OWN *WHEELS*...
...WHILE I GO ON FOOT!
ON YOUR MARK!

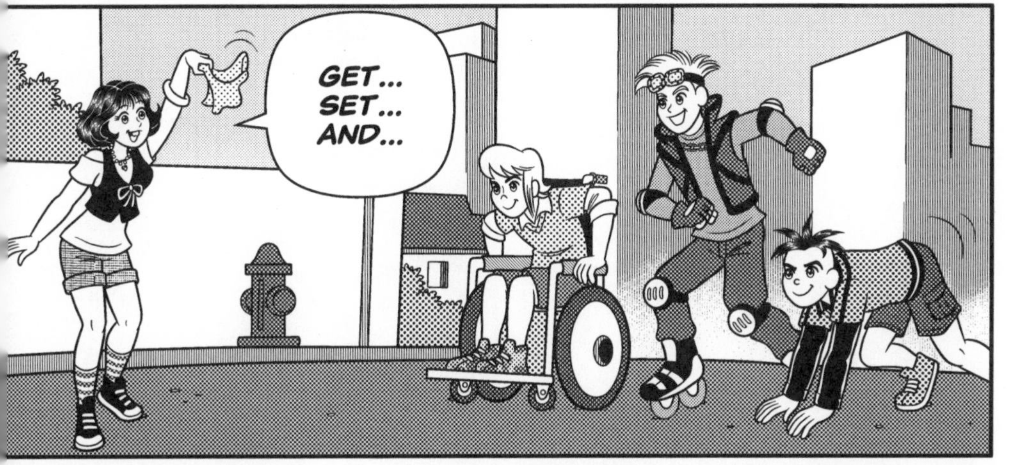
GET... SET... AND...

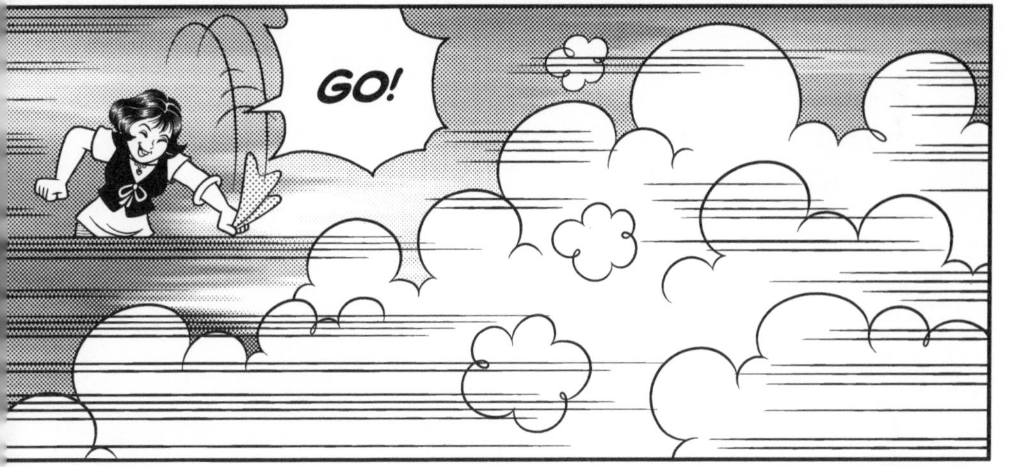
GO!

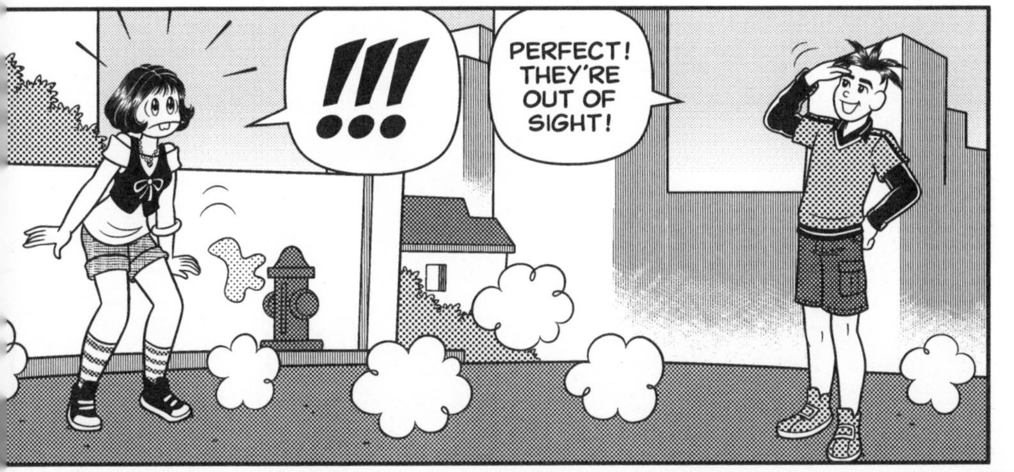
!!!
...
PERFECT! THEY'RE OUT OF SIGHT!

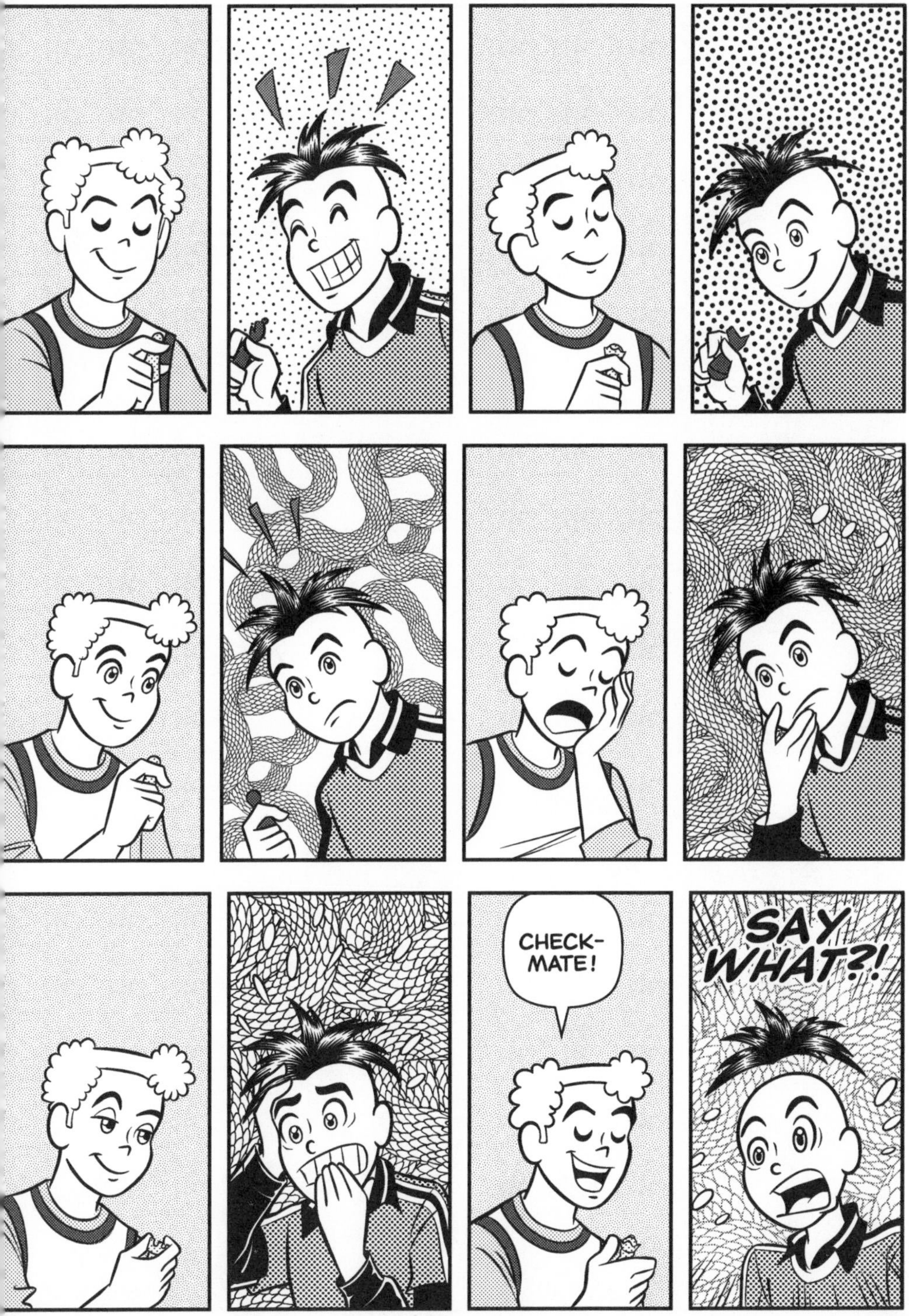
CHECK-
MATE!
SAY
WHAT?!

58

59

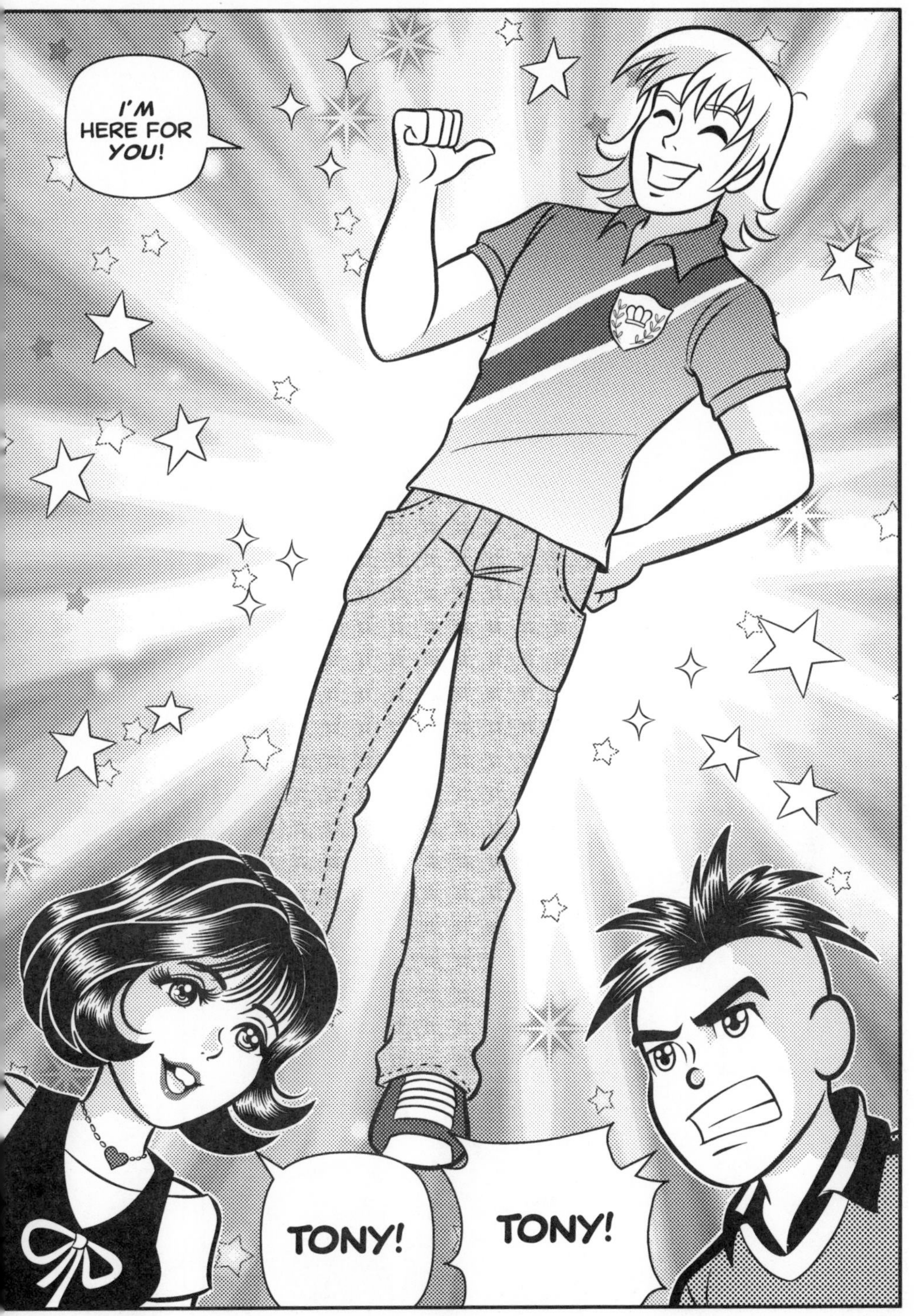
I'M HERE FOR YOU!
TONY!
TONY!

64

I'VE COME TO BE HER BOYFRIEND, NO LESS!

TONY?!

HA! YOU MUST BE JOKING!

HELP HER?! PROTECT HER?! YOU?! YOU ARE THE LEAST TRUSTWORTHY GUY IN THE ENTIRE NEIGHBORHOOD!

HAVE YOU *FORGOTTEN* WHAT THIS GUY DID, MONICA?!

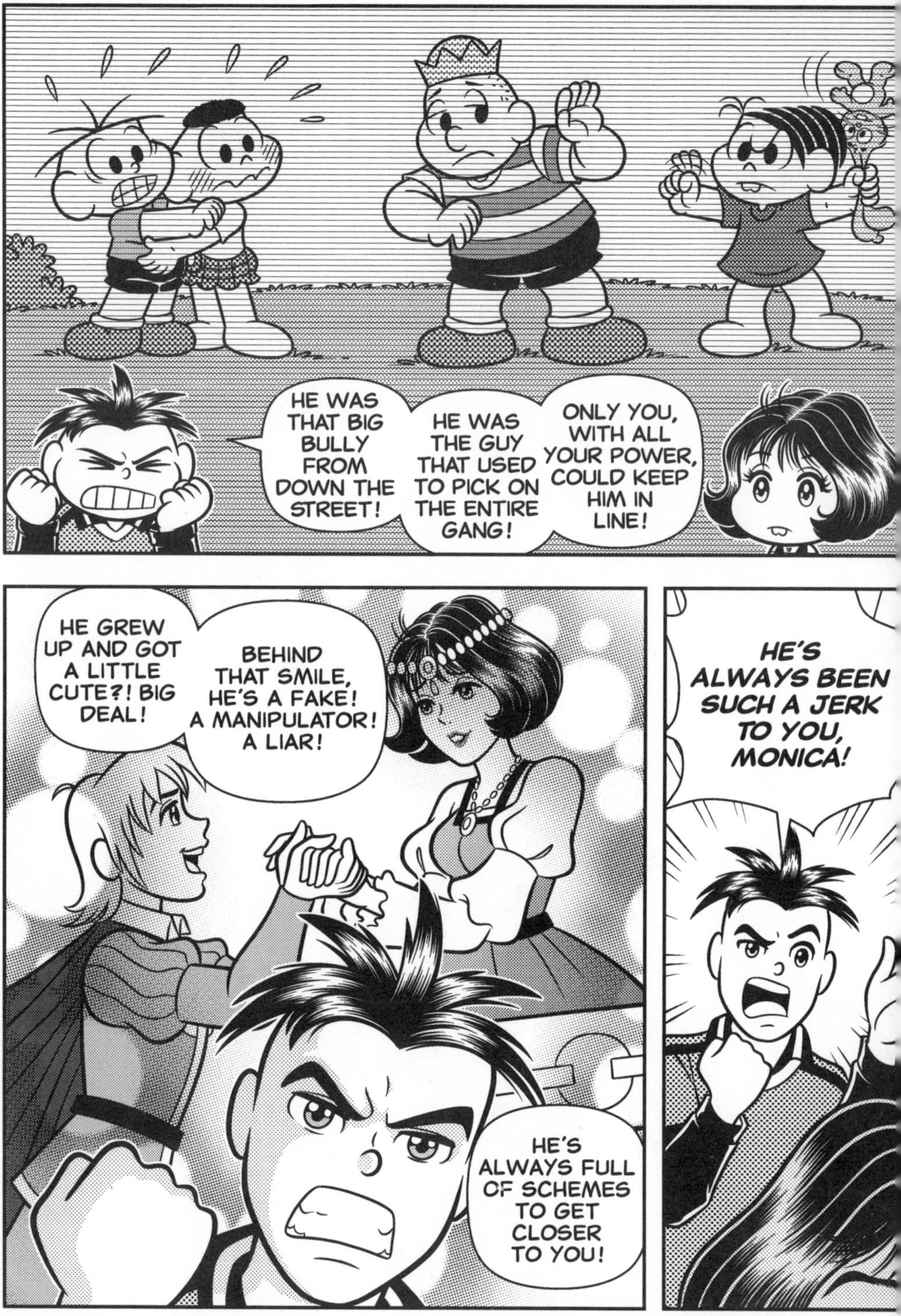
HE WAS THAT BIG BULLY FROM DOWN THE STREET!
HE WAS THE GUY THAT USED TO PICK ON THE ENTIRE GANG!
ONLY YOU, WITH ALL YOUR POWER, COULD KEEP HIM IN LINE!
HE GREW UP AND GOT A LITTLE CUTE?! BIG DEAL!
BEHIND THAT SMILE, HE'S A FAKE! A MANIPULATOR! A LIAR!
HE'S ALWAYS FULL OF SCHEMES TO GET CLOSER TO YOU!
HE'S ALWAYS BEEN SUCH A JERK TO YOU, MONICA!

69

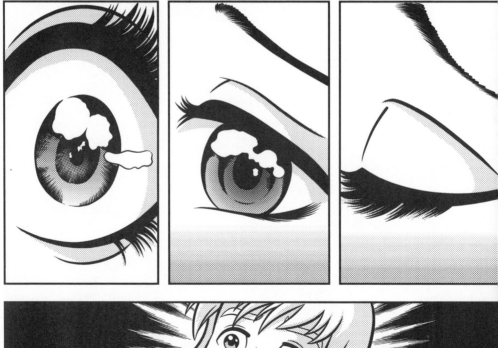

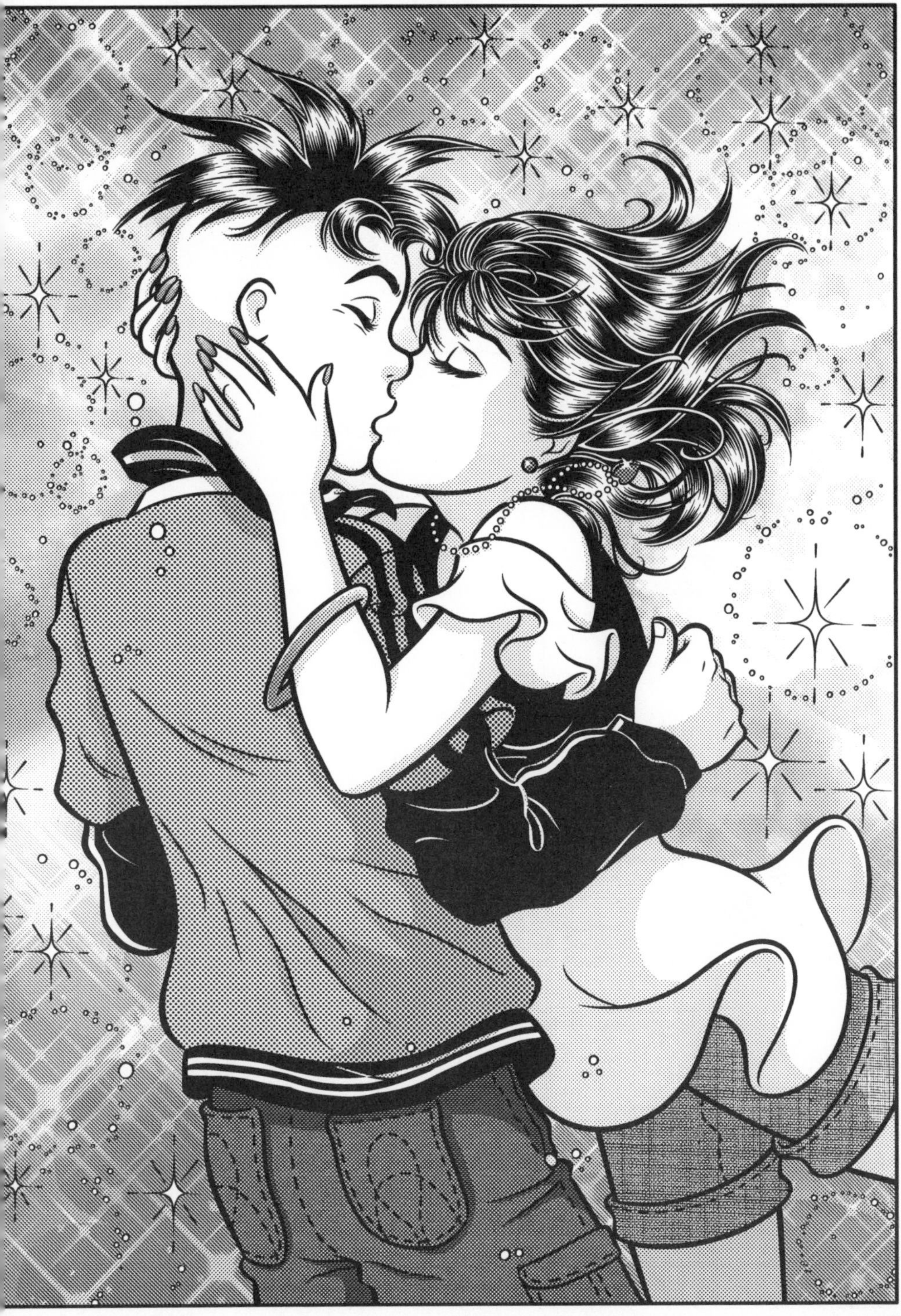

Finally, dating!

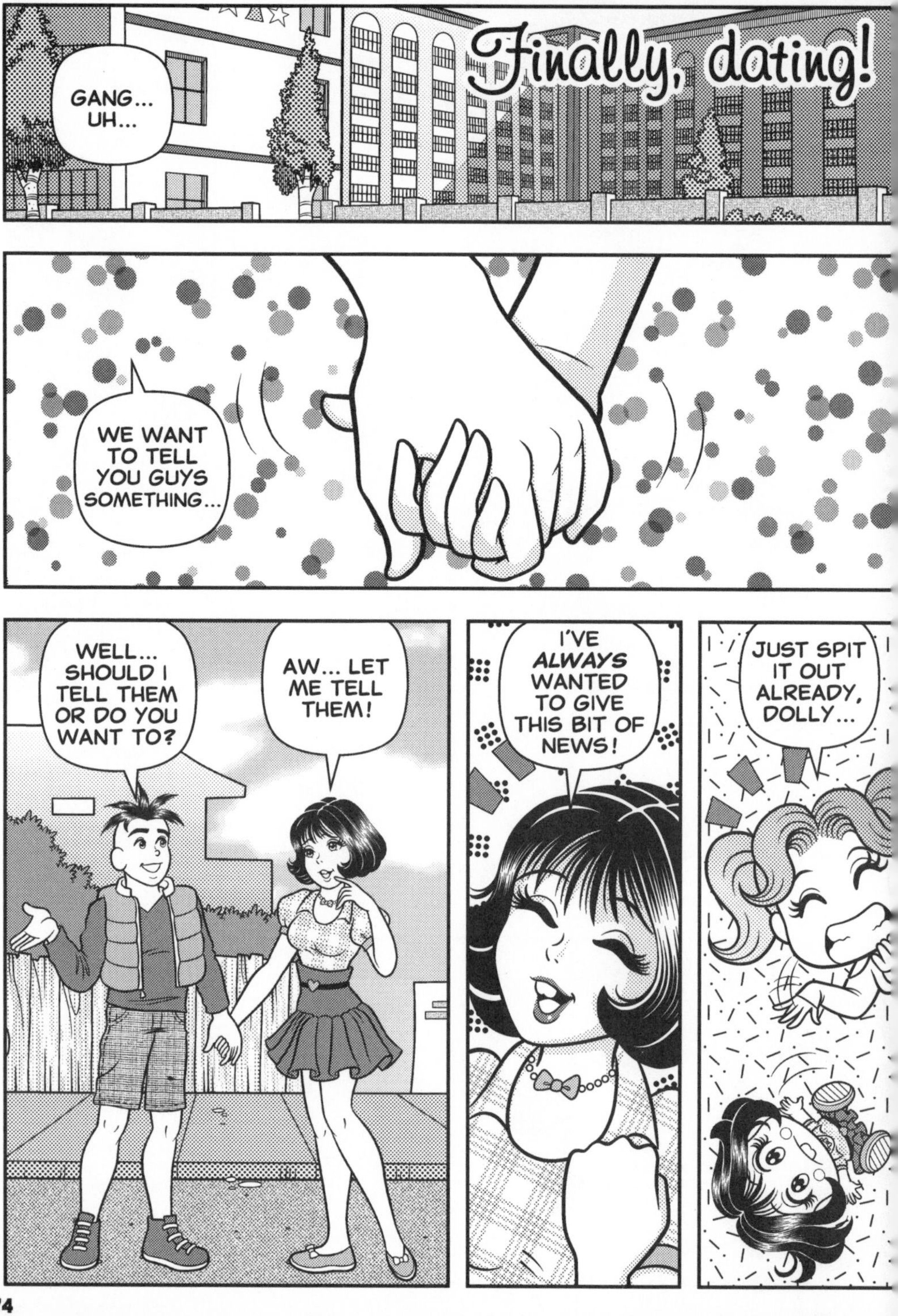

GANG... UH...
WE WANT TO TELL YOU GUYS SOMETHING...
WELL... SHOULD I TELL THEM OR DO YOU WANT TO?
AW... LET ME TELL THEM!
I'VE *ALWAYS* WANTED TO GIVE THIS BIT OF NEWS!
JUST SPIT IT OUT ALREADY, DOLLY...

82

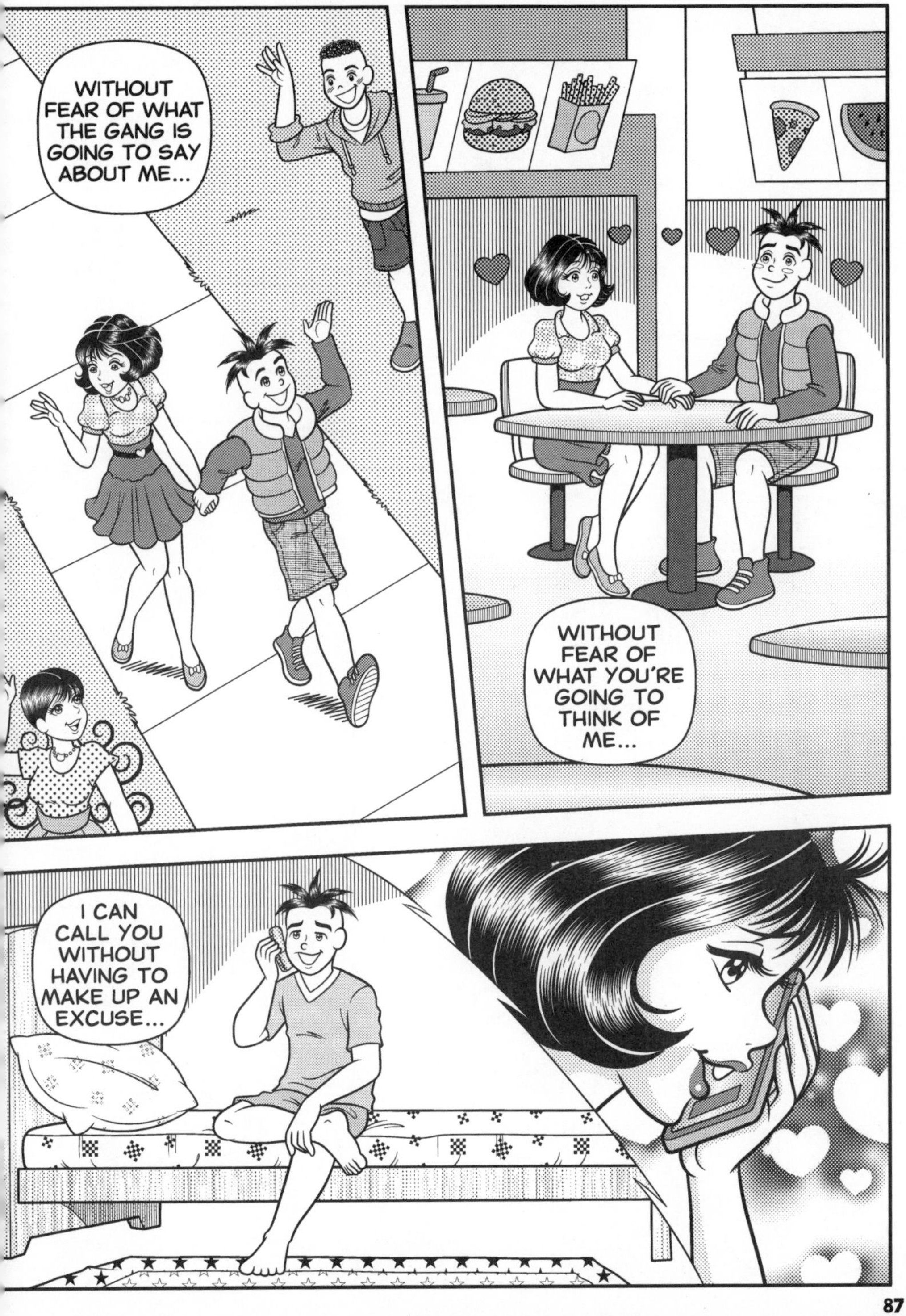
WITHOUT FEAR OF WHAT THE GANG IS GOING TO SAY ABOUT ME...
WITHOUT FEAR OF WHAT YOU'RE GOING TO THINK OF ME...
I CAN CALL YOU WITHOUT HAVING TO MAKE UP AN EXCUSE...

93

94

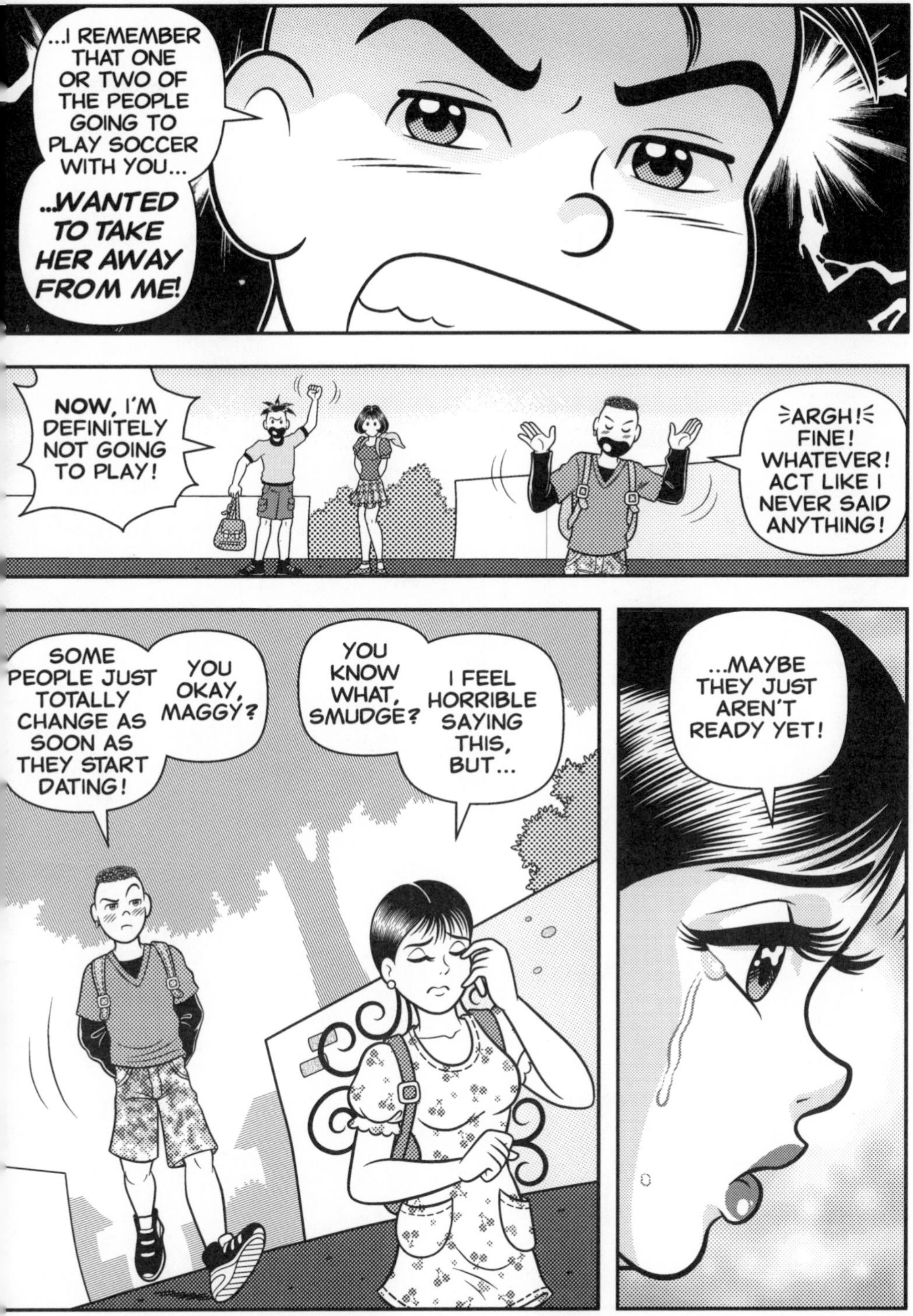
...I REMEMBER THAT ONE OR TWO OF THE PEOPLE GOING TO PLAY SOCCER WITH YOU...
...WANTED TO TAKE HER AWAY FROM ME!
NOW, I'M DEFINITELY NOT GOING TO PLAY!
ARGH! FINE! WHATEVER! ACT LIKE I NEVER SAID ANYTHING!
SOME PEOPLE JUST TOTALLY CHANGE AS SOON AS THEY START DATING!
YOU OKAY, MAGGY?
YOU KNOW WHAT, SMUDGE?
I FEEL HORRIBLE SAYING THIS, BUT...
...MAYBE THEY JUST AREN'T READY YET!

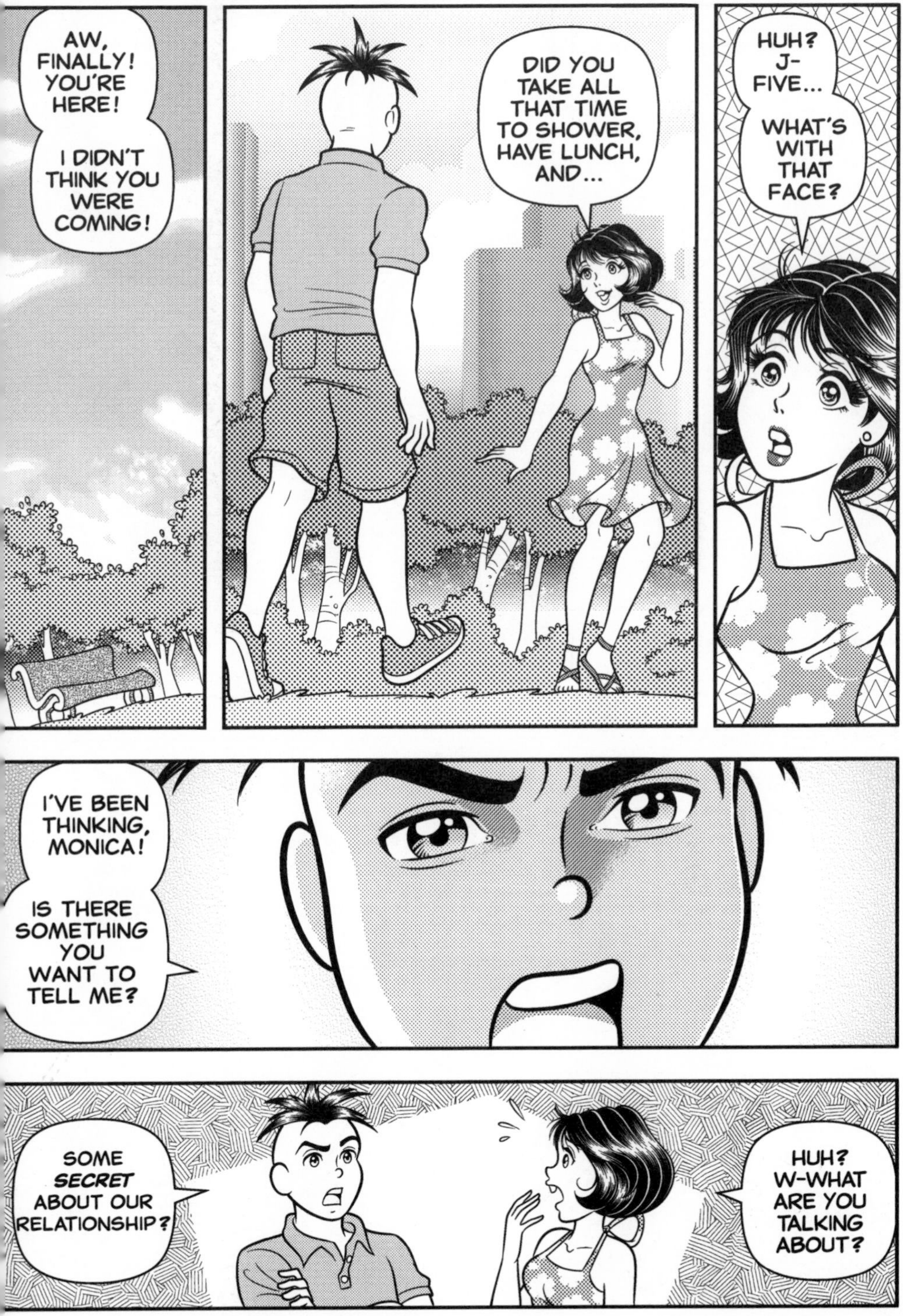
AW, FINALLY! YOU'RE HERE!
I DIDN'T THINK YOU WERE COMING!
DID YOU TAKE ALL THAT TIME TO SHOWER, HAVE LUNCH, AND...
HUH? J-FIVE...
WHAT'S WITH THAT FACE?
I'VE BEEN THINKING, MONICA!
IS THERE SOMETHING YOU WANT TO TELL ME?
SOME *SECRET* ABOUT OUR RELATIONSHIP?
HUH? W-WHAT ARE YOU TALKING ABOUT?

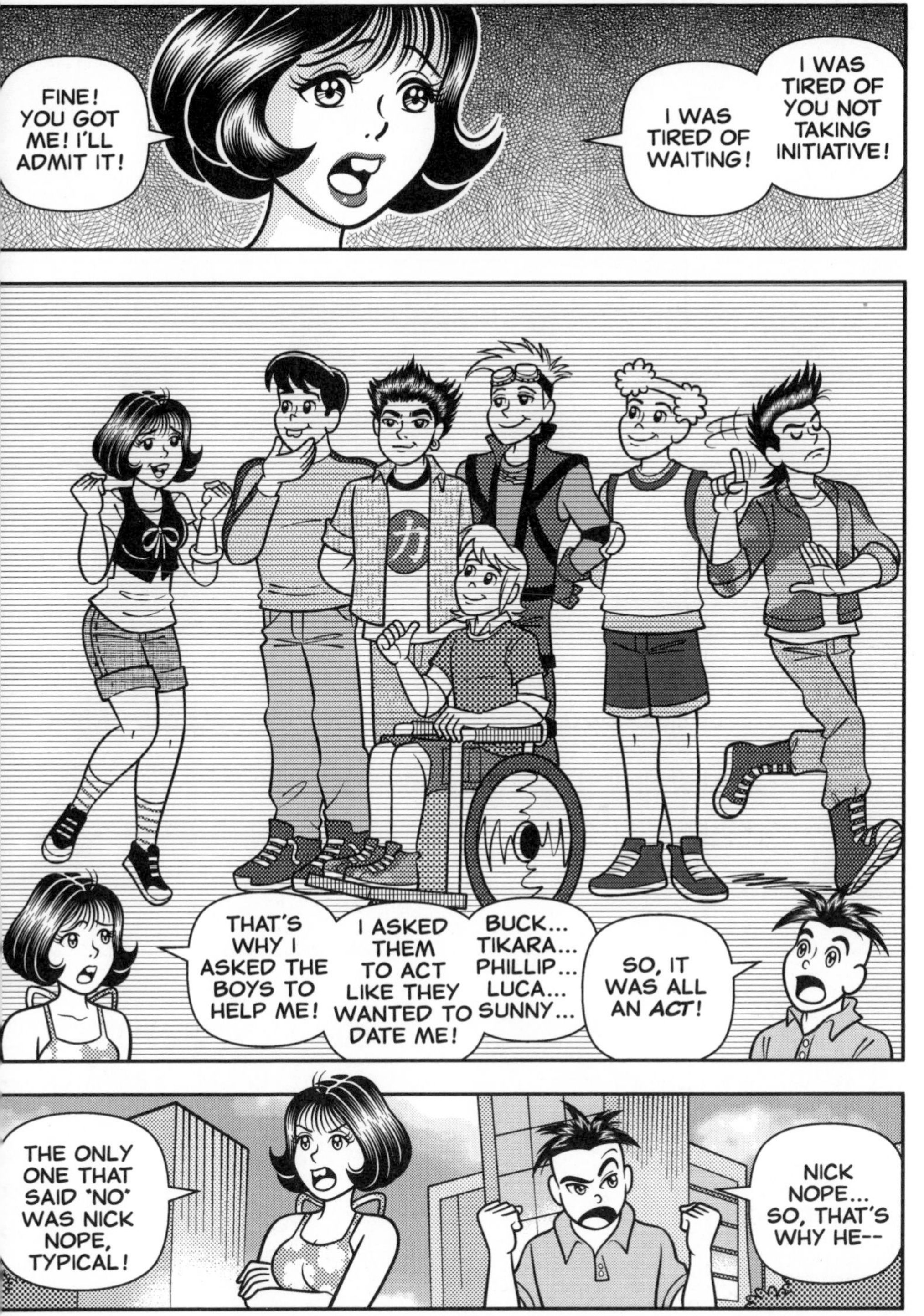
FINE! YOU GOT ME! I'LL ADMIT IT!
I WAS TIRED OF WAITING!
I WAS TIRED OF YOU NOT TAKING INITIATIVE!
THAT'S WHY I ASKED THE BOYS TO HELP ME!
I ASKED THEM TO ACT LIKE THEY WANTED TO DATE ME!
BUCK... TIKARA... PHILLIP... LUCA... SUNNY...
SO, IT WAS ALL AN *ACT*!
THE ONLY ONE THAT SAID "NO" WAS NICK NOPE, TYPICAL!
NICK NOPE... SO, THAT'S WHY HE--

...I LOVE YOU!

YOU KNOW WHAT ALL OF THIS MEANS, MONICA?!

WE ARE DONE!

DONE?! WHAT DO YOU MEAN, "DONE"? OUR RELATIONSHIP WAS PERFECT! AND YOU WERE HAPPY AND SATISFIED AND SWEET AND NOW YOU WANT TO END EVERYTHING OVER SOMETHING SO DUMB ABOUT DEFEATING ME?!

YOU MEAN, YOU DON'T LIKE ME ANYMORE?

YOU JUST WANTED TO BEAT ME AT SOMETHING?! THAT'S IT?!

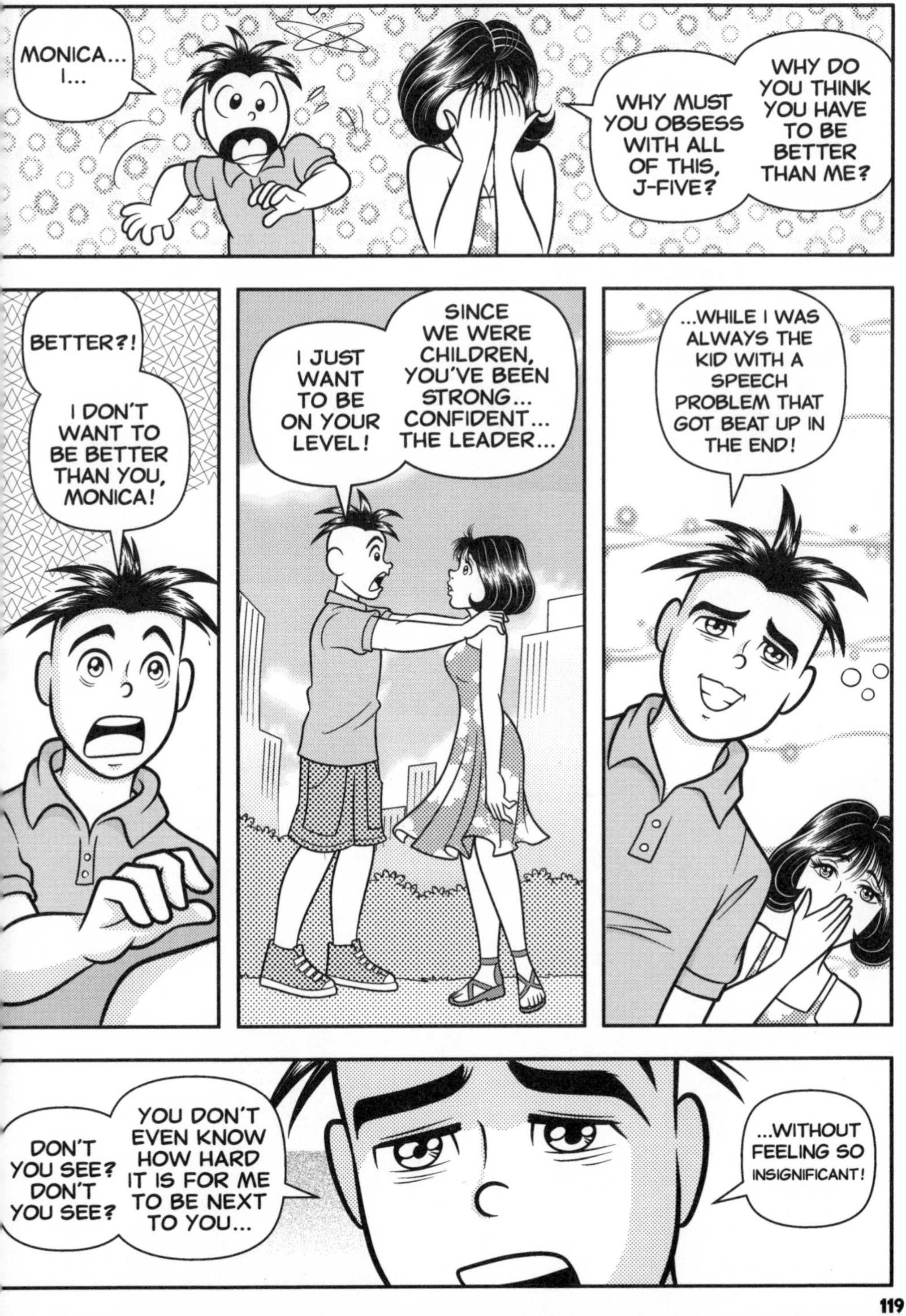
MONICA... I...
WHY MUST YOU OBSESS WITH ALL OF THIS, J-FIVE?
WHY DO YOU THINK YOU HAVE TO BE BETTER THAN ME?
BETTER?!
I DON'T WANT TO BE BETTER THAN YOU, MONICA!
I JUST WANT TO BE ON YOUR LEVEL!
SINCE WE WERE CHILDREN, YOU'VE BEEN STRONG... CONFIDENT... THE LEADER...
...WHILE I WAS ALWAYS THE KID WITH A SPEECH PROBLEM THAT GOT BEAT UP IN THE END!
DON'T YOU SEE? DON'T YOU SEE?
YOU DON'T EVEN KNOW HOW HARD IT IS FOR ME TO BE NEXT TO YOU...
...WITHOUT FEELING SO INSIGNIFICANT!

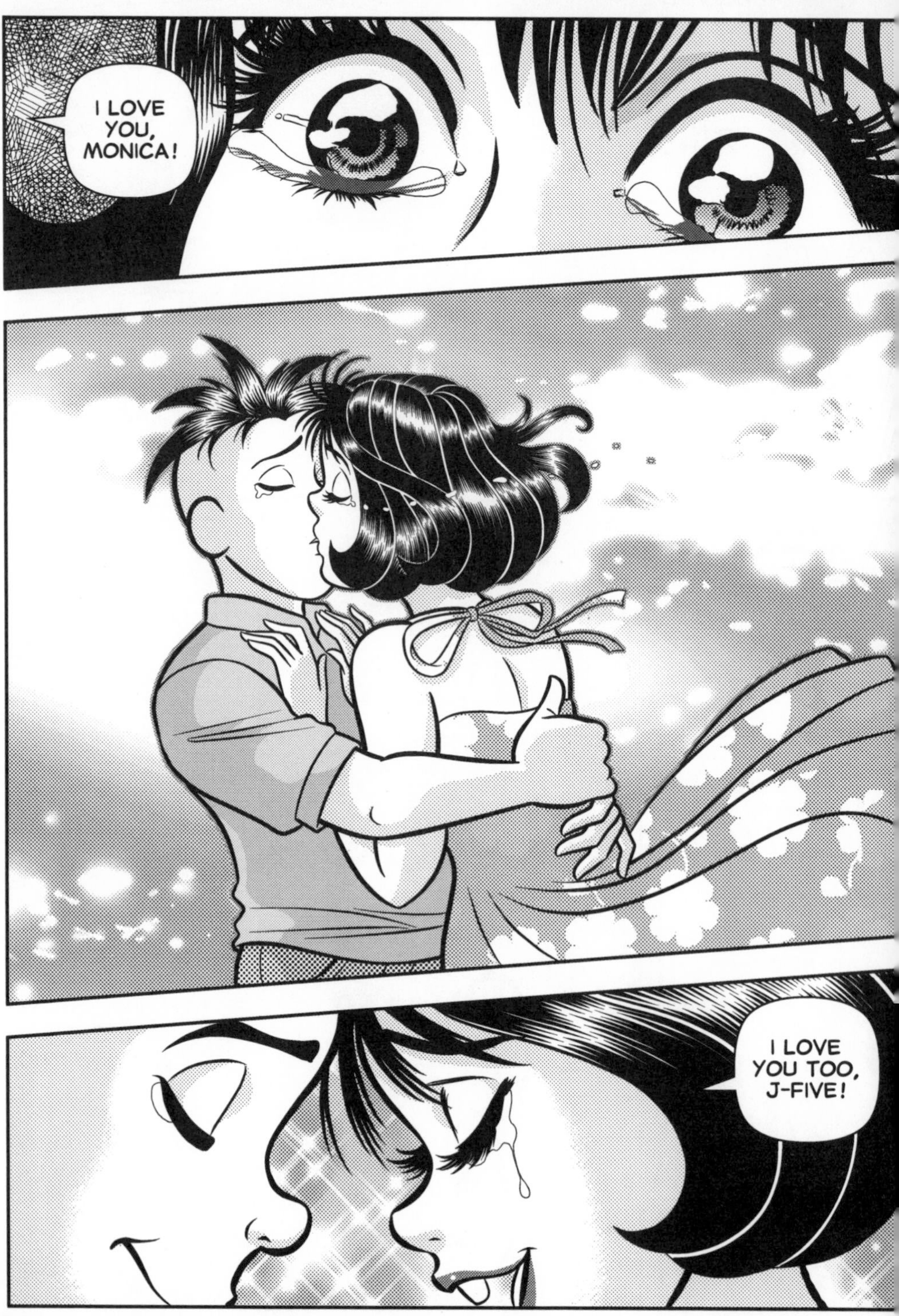
I LOVE YOU, MONICA!
I LOVE YOU TOO, J-FIVE!

MORE GRAPHIC NOVELS AVAILABLE FROM Charmz™

**STITCHED #1
"THE FIRST DAY OF THE
REST OF HER LIFE"**

**STITCHED #2
"LOVE IN THE TIME
OF ASSUMPTION"**

**G.F.F.s #1
"MY HEART LIES
IN THE 90s"**

**G.F.F.s #2
"WITCHES GET
THINGS DONE"**

**CHLOE #1
"THE NEW GIRL"**

**CHLOE #2 "THE QUEEN
OF HIGH SCHOOL"**

**CHLOE #3
"FRENEMIES"**

**CHLOE #4
"RAINY DAY"**

**SCARLET ROSE #1
"I KNEW I'D MEET YOU"**

**SCARLET ROSE #2
"I'LL GO WHERE YOU GO"**

**SCARLET ROSE #3
"I THINK I LOVE YOU"**

**SCARLET ROSE #4
"YOU WILL ALWAYS BE MINE"**

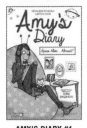

**AMY'S DIARY #1
"SPACE ALIEN...
ALMOST?"**

**SWEETIES #1
"CHERRY SKYE"**

MONICA ADVENTURES #1

**ANA AND THE
COSMIC RACE #1
"THE RACE BEGINS"**

Charmz graphic novels are available for $9.99 in paperback, and $14.99 in hardcover. Monica Adventures is available for $8.99 in paperback, and $13.99 hardcover. Available from booksellers everywhere.

You can also order online from www.papercutz.com. Or call 1-800-886-1223, Monday through Friday, 9–5 EST. MC, Visa, and AmEx accepted. To order by mail, please add $5.00 for postage and handling for first book ordered, $1.00 for each additional book and make check payable to NBM Publishing.
Send to: Charmz, 160 Broadway, Suite 700, East Wing, New York, NY 10038.
Charmz graphic novels are also available wherever e-books are sold.

Charmz chat™

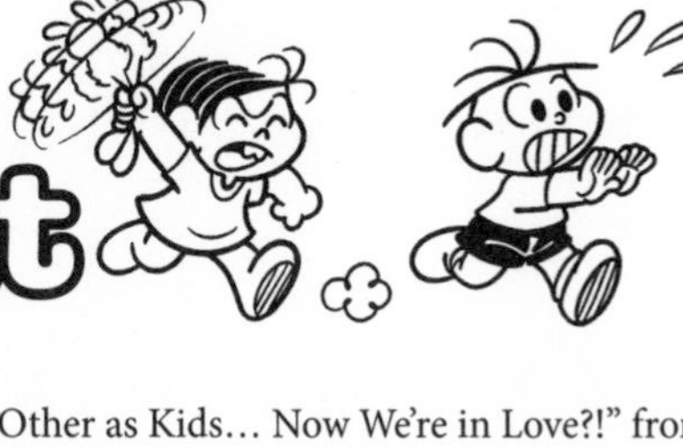

Welcome to MONICA ADVENTURES #2 "We Fought Each Other as Kids… Now We're in Love?!" from the crushing folks at Charmz, the Papercutz imprint devoted to romantic and fun graphic novels. We're thrilled to be able to bring one of the most popular comics characters in the world to North America—MONICA! Created by comics legend Mauricio de Sousa, who was inspired by his own daughter when she was a brash child. Monica the comics character therefore started as a child, and her best-selling comics series is still going strong today. In fact, Monica is still just a kid in her main comics series, but another comic was spun off, called MONICA TEEN, and those are the comics we're presenting here—starring the teenage Monica. Check out MONICA ADVENTURES #1 for a little more background on Mauricio and MONICA.

Here in MONICA ADVENTURES #2, we see longtime childhood rivals Monica and J-Five admitting their feelings for (and their mischievous plans against) one another! It's like watching a tennis match or a really exciting chess match as these two teens battle it out to try and control their hearts and emotions.

Monica and J-Five have been chasing after each other since her introduction in comics back in 1963 in Brazil. Monica appeared in the newspaper strip of J-Five (Cebolinha in Brazil). In that classic comic strip, Jimmy is trying to see how long he can balance on the sidewalk when he comes across Monica. He asks her to move. By the third panel, Monica was already whacking poor Jimmy with her plush bunny. Nursing his new black eye, he laments, "Now I know how women can trip up a guy!" Such was the beginning of a beautiful friendship. For years J-Five continues to try to one up Monica with his infallible plans, and doing silly things like stealing her bunny to tie knots in its ears. But the results would always be Monica returning, pounding Jimmy in fruitless attempts to teach him a lesson. But now that they're teenagers, all that has changed. The story in this landmark MONICA adventure brings their relationship to an important turning point. Everything is now different between these two childhood friends, and we can't wait to see what happens next. Someone who may know exactly what might happen next, offers his insights on all this…

A SPECIAL MESSAGE FROM
MAURICIO DE SOUSA
THE CREATOR OF MONICA

To date or not to date? To marry or not to marry? These are some of the doubts that we've questioned for a long time, especially after the launch of MONICA ADVENTURES. After all, when will J-Five and Monica finally fulfill whatever destiny awaits them? In this graphic novel, we gave a glimpse into what could be around the corner. Which begs the question, is marriage really the best option between these

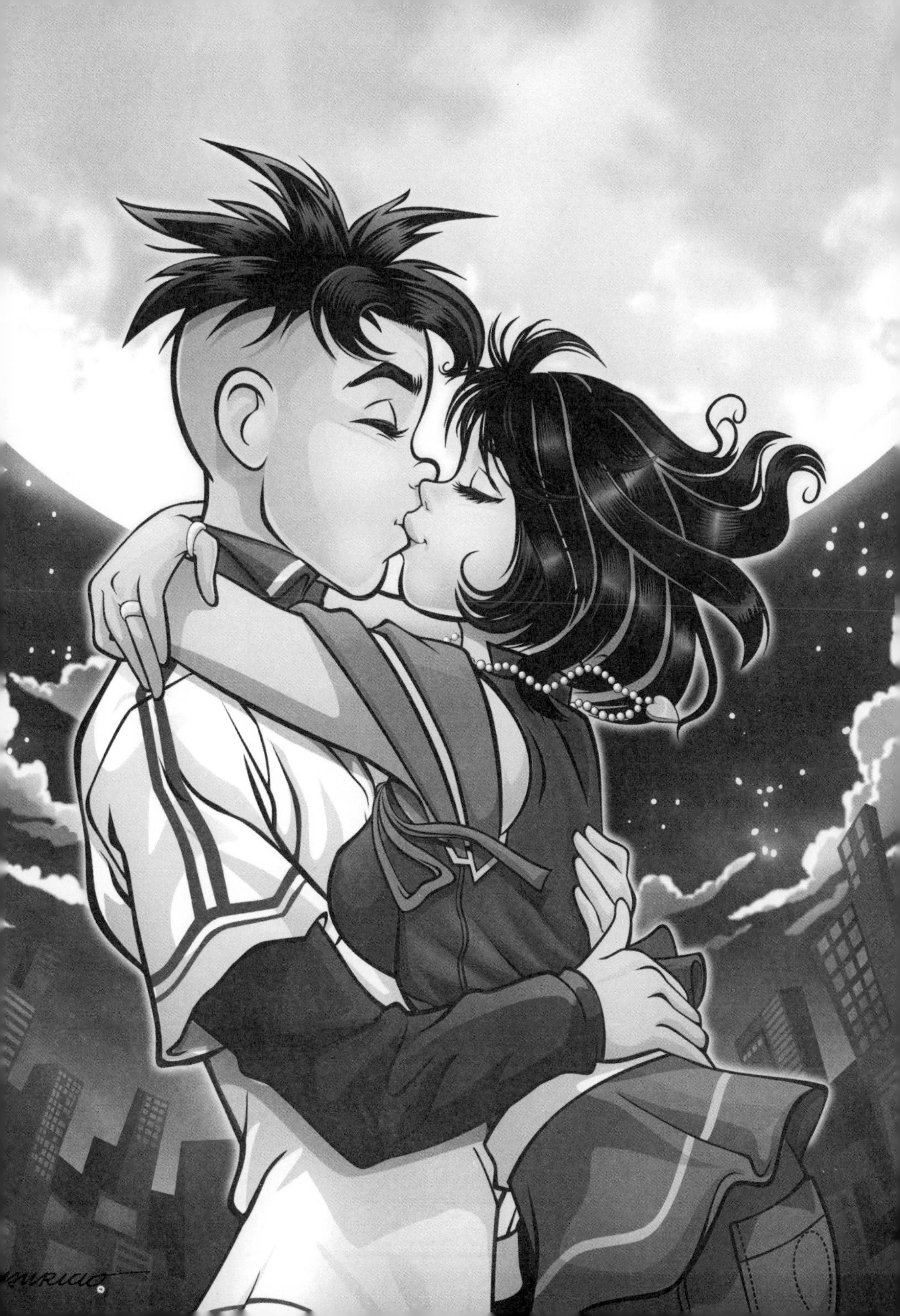

two characters? Let us reflect on other famous couples we know from comic strip history, couples that have had us cheering and hoping for a possible marriage, just like what many fans are wishing for Monica and J-Five.

There are many to choose from… From Superman and Lois Lane; The Phantom and his Diana; Mandrake the Magician and the enteral Narda; Tarzan from the wild and the civilized Jane; Prince Valiant and the beautiful princess Aleta; Li'l Abner and Daisy Mae; Popeye and Olive Oyl; Mickey and his match, Minnie; Donald Duck and Daisy Duck; Flash Gordon accompanied by Dale Arden; there's Alley Oop and Ooola; Will Eisner's The Spirit and his love interest Ellen, Commissioner Dolan's daughter; and many, many more that wouldn't even fit on this page. Some of them got married after years and years of flirting with the idea.

But… have you ever noticed? The ones that did get married in a hurry lost presence in the newspapers and magazines they used to frequent. Disappeared. Does that mean that marriage is unfit for comicbook duos? A thesis could be discussed and debated. And so, while we do research and study this phenomenon, it would be best to think twice about the future romance between Monica and J-Five! We can continue to cheer for a happy ending, but… what is a happy ending for a comicbook couple? P.S. – Is it true that happy endings, like a marriage, just don't sell well?

Mauricio
Mauricio de Sousa

We at Charmz desperately want to believe in true love. Charmz Editor-in-Chief Jim Salicrup was the Marvel editor when the Amazing Spider-Man and his love Mary Jane married many years ago. More recently Editor Jeff Whitman brought back Gumby's girlfriend Tara, in stories he wrote for the graphic novel GUMBY #1 "Fifty Shades of Clay" from Papercutz. And to be fair to Mauricio's point, Marvel Comics, in its infinite wisdom, undid the Spider-Man wedding (It never happened according to current continuity, although we hear Peter and MJ are dating again) in the comics (They're still married in the newspaper strip) and despite all our efforts, our GUMBY comic didn't exactly break any sales records. Still, we are true believers, and wish Monica and J-Five the best in the future. We are looking forward to being along for the ride in all the ups and downs of their relationship.

COMING SOON: Did you happen to notice that Nick Nope seemed determined to do something unexpected? We will see more of him (and his intentions) in future volumes of MONICA ADVENTURES. Coming up next is MONICA ADVENTURES #3 "Who's Saying Mean Things About Me… Online?!" Will Monica break the Internet? If any comicbook character could, it would be her!

STAY IN TOUCH!

EMAIL: whitman@papercutz.com
WEB: Papercutz.com
TWITTER: @papercutzgn
INSTAGRAM: @papercutzgn
FACEBOOK: PAPERCUTZGRAPHICNOVELS
FANMAIL: Charmz, 160 Broadway, Suite 700, East Wing, New York, NY 10038

31901064280508